Match of Death

It was football that put me in jail. More than that: it got me sentenced to death! . . . What is my crime? I scored a goal.

Vova is fifteen when the Nazis invade Kiev in 1941. He is only interested in playing football, but no one can stay on the sidelines in war. Vova and his sister join the partisans and do what they can to harass the enemy. But they soon realize that they are not only fighting the Germans but their own people too, the *Ountsi*—Ukrainians who have thrown in their lot with the Germans, splitting families apart to fight on different sides.

And then Vova is given the chance to play football again, against a German side. Only in this match the stakes are high: if Vova's team win, they will be shot. As Vova plays in this Match of Death he has to decide whether to disgrace his country and lose the game or win—and die.

This story is based on actual events that happened during the Nazi invasion of the Ukraine in the Second World War. For the book, the author interviewed in Kiev sons of dead footballers and eyewitnesses to the 'Match of Death'.

James Riordan was born in Portsmouth during the war. He had various jobs before doing his National Service in the RAF. After demobilization he gained degrees from Birmingham, London, and Moscow, then worked as a translator in Moscow. Back in England he lectured at Portsmouth Polytechnic and Birmingham and Bradford universities and at Surrey University where he was Professor of Russian Studies. He has written over twenty academic books on Russian social issues and on sport, several collections of folk-tales, and a number of picture books. *Sweet Clarinet* was his first novel for children; it won the 1999 NASEN Award and was shortlisted for the Whitbread Children's Book Award. *Match of Death* is his fifth novel for Oxford University Press.

Other Oxford books by James Riordan

Sweet Clarinet
The Prisoner
When the Guns Fall Silent
War Song
The Cello

Korean Folk-tales
Russian Folk-tales
Pinocchio
Gulliver's Travels
King Arthur
The Young Oxford Book of Football Stories
The Young Oxford Book of War Stories
The Young Oxford Book of Sports Stories

Match of Death

James Riordan

OXFORD
UNIVERSITY PRESS

OXFORD

UNIVERSITY PRESS

Great Clarendon Street, Oxford OX2 6DP

Oxford University Press is a department of the University of Oxford.
It furthers the University's objective of excellence in research, scholarship,
and education by publishing worldwide in

Oxford New York
Auckland Bangkok Buenos Aires
Cape Town Chennai Dar es Salaam Delhi Hong Kong Istanbul
Karachi Kolkata Kuala Lumpur Madrid Melbourne Mexico City Mumbai
Nairobi São Paulo Shanghai Taipei Tokyo Toronto

Oxford is a registered trade mark of Oxford University Press
in the UK and in certain other countries

British Library Cataloguing in Publication Data available

ISBN 0 19 275268 5

1 3 5 7 9 10 8 6 4 2

Typeset by AFS Image Setters Ltd, Glasgow
Printed in Great Britain by Cox & Wyman Ltd, Reading, Berks

To the memory of the Dinamo Kiev footballers executed
by the Nazis in 1942: Nikolai Trusevich,
Alexander Klimenko, Vladimir Kuzmenko, and
Nikolai Korotkikh.

This story is based on actual events that occurred during
the Nazi occupation of Kiev in World War Two. In the
war the Soviet Union lost 44 million people, of whom
one third were Ukrainians—some 15 million men,
women, and children. Such huge losses were far greater
than those of any other nation. Over 100,000 starved to
death in Kiev alone.

The football match took place between Kiev and
German players on 9 August 1942.

'You only live once. And you should live your life so that, dying, you can say: I gave everything to the people.'

Nikolai Ostrovsky, *How the Steel Was Tempered*

1

Life's like football.

Being in the right place at the right time. That can make you a hero. Score a goal, you win. Save a goal, you survive.

The Game of Life.

But, if you're in the wrong place at the wrong time . . . Bad luck, you miss out.

Death or Glory.

Coach says I'm a natural goalscorer, born with quick feet and brain. And he should know. He was once captain of the national team—football in summer, ice hockey in winter. A real all-rounder and National Hero.

Now he trains our Dinamo Kiev club.

In another time and place I could have been a star; maybe gone on to play for my country. Just think of that! I might have travelled abroad, been cheered on by thousands of fans, earned enough to look after Mum and Dad, and my three sisters.

Not now. This is wartime. No time for games.

My home town is Kiev, capital of the Ukraine. If you look it up on the map, you'll see we're on the route from Berlin to Moscow. So we stood in the way of the German army's march on the Soviet capital.

Now we're occupied by German troops, under the Nazi jackboot.

That's what I mean by being in the wrong place at the wrong time. If I'd been born in Timbuktu or Washington, I'd be safe. Mind you, I might not have played football . . .

It was football that put me in jail. More than that: it got me sentenced to death!

So here I sit on my wooden bunk, writing down my story. I hope I finish it before they lead me out to the city square. Hangman's Square we call it now.

The Gestapo like an audience, like the public to witness what they do to those who defy them. There's nothing better than stringing up young boys, watching them cry, kick, and squirm till their necks snap, and they swing slowly to and fro, to and fro, like willow branches in the breeze.

Swine. Heartless swine! We hate them as much as they hate us.

How can the nation that gave the world Mozart and Beethoven be so brutal, so inhuman, so cruel?

I'm sitting in my cell because there's barely room to stand, let alone walk. Four paces from cell door to far wall. I pace them out: four steps forward, four steps back. I stretch out my arms and touch the ceiling and opposite wall.

It's more like a stone coffin than a prison cell.

Despite the bright summer sun outside, here it's dark and damp. It stinks of pig shit. There's no window to let in light. Just four iron bars in the iron door through which a bare corridor lamp in an iron holder glimmers. Five narrow shafts of yellow light.

Like a stone overcoat all about me are rough-hewn walls pitted with words by former inmates—some etched by broken fingernail, some daubed in blood:

LONG LIVE VICTORY!

BYE, MUM.

MAYA

I DIE FOR STALIN

TRUTH AND FREEDOM

Someone had scratched a poem.

2

Wait for me and I'll return,
Wait while rivers run.
Wait when others wait no more,
When no letters come.
Wait with hope that never fades,
Wait and don't give in . . .
Wait

Caught in the act? Dragged off before he could finish it? Or, maybe, he saw no point in waiting.

Last words. Of those who died for truth and freedom. Or perhaps they were traitors. Who knows? Walls can't speak. Walls have ears but no mouths. And eyes on these walls are soon to close forever.

Now and again, mostly at night, a scream shatters the silence and shots ring out. Someone's got it in the neck! For resisting Germans. For being communists, gypsies, Slavs, Jews. For having black hair—or red. For being suntanned—or pasty-faced. For having too much money—or not enough.

As for me, I'm neither gypsy nor Jew. I'm plain old Ukrainian, third generation of once-proud Cossacks. At sixteen, I'm too young to be in the Communist Party. And I've fair hair and blue eyes—'like sun-bleached clouds in a summer sky', as my mother says.

To them, though, I'm a Slav, a slave, a worm to be squashed underfoot, a runt in the human litter. And runts are best put down. They make the world untidy for the Master Race.

The jailers—the *Hilfi*, our own Ukrainian flesh and blood—treat me like dirt, worse than a partisan. At mealtimes I get cabbage water and rock hard bread, matchbox size. They allow me out briefly once a day, to empty my slop pail into the prison sewer. Then I have to brave kicks and curses from the jailers, and even fellow prisoners who blame me for making their lives worse.

But the faces of my team-mates and other patriots light up with pride when they see me. And they fill me with that same hope and courage I give them.

I know I did right.

What is my crime?

I scored a goal.

Let me tell you how it came about.

2

It all started a year ago, in the Moscow Kremlin.

The war was going badly. Nazi Germany had invaded at dawn on 22 June 1941, and soon overran much of our country, just as it had the rest of Europe. Within three months, the German army had taken Kiev and was at the gates of Moscow. It had surrounded Leningrad and blitzed its way through the west of the Soviet Union.

One more push and we'd fall into their laps, like rotten fruit from a rotten tree.

Or so Hitler thought.

But he was wrong.

Stalin was plotting his downfall. He had called an emergency meeting.

As usual, he sat in the shadows at one end of the oval table, puffing quietly on his pipe, like a wise old patriarch. He was wearing his simple grey army uniform, though it was badly crumpled as if he'd been sleeping in it. Even his thick grey speckled moustache drooped, to match his sombre mood. A dark hank of hair overhung his swarthy pock-marked face.

To those who didn't know him he looked a beaten man.

It was his henchman, NKVD security chief Beria, bald and thin-lipped, who opened the meeting. He peered through his pebble glasses at the three others round the table: Chief of Staff Zhukov, Foreign Minister Molotov, and Sports Minister Colonel Snegov.

'Comrades, it is no secret that morale is low. The Fascist occupation has taken its toll. Our glorious Red

5

Army has already lost more men than any army in history, and many traitors have gone over to the enemy.'

'Like rats fleeing a sinking ship,' muttered Molotov.

'The ship is *not* sinking!' barked Zhukov. 'We have halted the German advance . . . At Leningrad, at Moscow, at Stalingrad. The tide will turn.'

'If only the Allies would open a second front, invade northern France,' said Molotov with a sigh. 'It would take some of the heat off us.'

Stalin's yellow wolf eyes flashed, but he said nothing.

Noticing Stalin's look, Beria rounded on Molotov.

'If you trust Britain like you trusted Germany when you signed that useless pact with Ribbentrop, you're a bloody fool. No, we are alone, we can't rely on outside help. It's us against Germany, communism against capitalism.

'To win *we must raise morale! Understand?*'

He uttered the last words in a hoarse whisper that threatened each of the ministers. His cold eyes searched their faces. He knew, they knew, he held their lives in his hands. They kept silent.

'We'll leave war fronts aside for the moment. It's the home front that concerns us here: lifting our people's spirits.'

The Sports Minister, who had wondered why on earth he had been summoned, ventured a word.

'The masses love sport. It gives them hope. Do you recall last May's football match in Leningrad? Amid the shells and bombs? We broadcast the game all along the front; every soldier listened in. Football takes people's minds off the war.'

Beria said coldly, 'No one's mind must be taken off the war! Even sports ministers ought to remember that!'

Colonel Snegov paled, recalling the fate of previous sports chiefs—shot or sent to labour camps for *not* remembering, or for remembering too much . . .

6

'But you're right about football raising morale,' Beria continued. 'Our wise leader Generalissimo Stalin has a plan.'

All eyes turned to the Supreme Commander.

But he was in no hurry to speak. Taking the pipe from his lips, he knocked out the spent tobacco ash, then sat back calmly in his chair. After fixing his dull eyes on each of them in turn, he leaned forward and put his hands on the table.

Then he spoke quietly, in a Russian heavy with his southern accent.

'He who takes up the sword against us shall perish by the sword. On that the lands of Rus will always stand. This is *total war*, a choice between freedom or slavery.'

Turning to Beria, he suddenly asked, 'Lavrenty Pavlovich, you once played football, I believe?'

He didn't wait for confirmation.

'You played dirty even then. Never mind, football can be a handy weapon. In war it can be more important than life itself. We will use it to give a death-dealing blow to the enemy.'

He looked round the table with a wolfish smile.

'We shall organize a Match of Death!' he hissed.

Without waiting for his words to sink in, he continued, 'Us against Germany. In occupied Kiev. Our victory will show the world that the Germans *can* be beaten!'

When no further details issued from under the drooping moustache, the others—all except Zhukov— gave enthusiastic nods of approval. For the life of them, however, they didn't see how the Germans would let a starving rag-bag of footballers beat them.

Molotov nervously made a suggestion.

'Comrade Stalin is a genius. That is a truly brilliant plan. To ensure victory, perhaps we might send reinforcements, our best players—like Moscow Spartak's Starostin brothers . . . '

His words tailed off as he felt Stalin's eyes boring into him. Beria hurriedly whispered in his ear.

'They were arrested last year for plotting to kill Comrade Stalin. You remember, during the match on Red Square. The football was really a bomb!'

Red-faced, Molotov looked down at the polished table.

Zhukov, however, was the one man present unafraid of the Great Genius and Generalissimo. And now he muttered, 'More lambs to the slaughter . . . '

Uncertain to whom he was referring—the Starostin brothers or the Kiev footballers—the others looked towards Comrade Stalin. But the Great Leader was silent.

'And how will a football match help us win the war?' demanded Zhukov. 'If your football tactics are no better than your military tactics, we'll lose the match *and* the war!'

Instead of flying into a rage at this slight, Stalin smiled craftily.

'I know what you're thinking, comrades. The Fascists would win. Yes, yes, of course they would! And the propaganda victory would be theirs. No, comrades, the match will *not* be played in Kiev. It will be *here*, in Moscow, behind closed doors.'

Their looks of astonishment amused him.

'Both teams will be *ours*: Reds—the Soviet Union, Whites—Germany. We shall broadcast the game throughout the country—and beyond—*as if it were a real match*, live from Kiev.'

He sat back, refilled the pipe with his favourite Golden Fleece tobacco, and allowed a flicker of a smile to play on his lips.

'The Match of Death!'

The words hissed out in a cloud of blue smoke.

'Of course, we'll have the Fascists order our players to lose on pain of death. But our lads will defy them, and die for their country.'

Colonel Snegov could not contain himself.

'A truly marvellous idea. We'll plan it down to the last detail. The Writers Union can write the script, our esteemed theatre director Meyerhold can stage the match . . .'

The atmosphere grew tense again. This time it was Molotov who broke the news.

'Colonel Snegov, as a sports official, you may not be aware that your "esteemed" Meyerhold has been shot as an enemy of the people.'

Molotov knew better than most how Stalin and Beria had tortured and shot thousands of their own people. He still kept a letter smuggled out of prison from Meyerhold just before his death.

'I appeal to you, Comrade Molotov. I'm a sick old man. Yet they force me to lie face down and then beat my back and the soles of my feet with a rubber strap. When I'm covered in bruises they beat the bruises. It's like having boiling water poured over you . . . Then they punch me in the face as hard as they can. Death is easier than this. I confess to any nonsense so as to get it over with as quickly as possible.'

Molotov had done nothing. What could he do? No one could reason with Stalin. And Beria was just a vicious thug. It didn't surprise Molotov that he'd played football: one of those who elbowed opponents in the face and kicked their shins when the ref's back was turned.

As for Stalin, no pity could be expected there. Even when the Germans had captured his son Yakov, he'd refused their offer to swap him for a German prisoner. A month later the Germans had shot Yakov. No one could tell from the father's stony face whether he cared or not.

'That's settled then,' declared Stalin abruptly. 'The match will be played on 9 August 1942.'

The script would be written, the score decided beforehand. And each minister would do his bit to give the game utmost publicity at home and abroad.

The Match of Death would be a brilliant propaganda coup.

3

Berlin, February 1942.

The German Supreme Commander Adolf Hitler had summoned a meeting of top Nazi officials to discuss a secret report. Sitting round the table were Gestapo chief Heinrich Himmler, Propaganda Minister Joseph Goebbels, and Field Marshall Hermann Goering.

Hitler opened the meeting. He was clearly in happy mood, rubbing his hands and beaming with joy.

'Gentlemen! The war is going well. Our victorious armies have fought their way to the Atlantic in the west, to the Alps in the south, to the Baltic in the north; and they are on the march to the Pacific in the east. Only the British hold us up in the west. But once we have dealt with the Russians, we will invade England—and all Europe will be ours. Nothing is impossible for the German soldier!

'Then we will rid the world of communists and Jews, like pruning a tree of dead wood. We will remove all Slavs to beyond the Ural Mountains, to the Slavlands, and populate the cleared area with Germans, giving them room to live and breathe.

'Then the great German nation will rule Europe, bring order in place of chaos. We Aryans will no longer have to live cheek by jowl with sewer rats and cripples . . . '

He was getting into his stride, his voice rasping like an angry wasp about their ears. His colleagues had heard it all before. They were used to the Führer ranting and raving for hours, his hoarse voice rising to fever pitch, as if he were addressing the masses at some vast stadium rally.

Goebbels and Himmler seemed not to hear; they stared

straight ahead across the long oak table, waiting for the storm to blow itself out. Goering, resplendent in white air force uniform, was too bored to suffer these rantings. He had come prepared, with wads of cotton wool stuffed firmly into his ears.

An hour later, the waves had crashed up the shore to the high tide mark, and they were beginning to roll out to sea again. At last, some time between pounding the table with his fists and wiping his small black moustache, Hitler's mouth ran dry and he rang a brass handbell.

As if from nowhere, two maids in black dress, white apron, and frilly lace cap appeared with trays of tea.

While the three men clapped politely, and Himmler and Goebbels raised their right arms, barking 'Sieg Heil!', Goering quietly removed the ear plugs.

After sipping his tea, Hitler cleared his throat. His next words took the company by surprise.

'How many press-ups did you do this morning?'

His gaze passed from the podgy, sweating Goering to the weedy, short-sighted figures of Himmler and Goebbels.

Without waiting for an answer, Hitler said sternly, 'I expect all Nazi leaders to show an example to the German people. A healthy mind in a healthy body. Through fitness and sport we demonstrate the superiority of our race; we display the spartan spirit of Ancient Greece.

'Sport and war go hand in hand. Our sportsmen are soldiers in tracksuits, fighting for the Fatherland. He who wins the race, wins the war. Right, Herr Himmler?'

Himmler adjusted his glasses, glanced down at the report before him and took up the cue.

'Absolutely right, *mein Führer*. May I report?'

Hitler nodded curtly, one side of his neatly-parted hair flopping over his brow.

'Through our spies in Moscow we have learned of a

dastardly Russian plot. They are planning a football match, code-named the "Match of Death". In August, Germany will play the Soviet Union. Of course, the Russians intend to win.'

He gave a bitter laugh.

'It will be a circus of clowns staged secretly in Moscow, with commentary broadcast all over Russia—as if the match is taking place in Kiev, arranged by us.'

Hitler broke in, unable to contain himself.

'We must deprive Stalin of a propaganda victory. Germany *cannot* be beaten! Germany will *not* be beaten. *Never!*'

His voice rose to the rafters again and he banged the table with his fist, making the teacups rattle. Rounding on Goebbels, he cried, 'What do *you* say, Herr Goebbels?'

'Naturally, *mein Führer*. We will not be beaten. We will turn the tables, seize the initiative and stage the match in Kiev ourselves. We will send a crack SS team to ensure victory and broadcast Germany's triumph to the whole world.

'German sports power is famed throughout the globe. Everyone knows the Berlin Olympics were the greatest ever. Did we not win more medals than any other nation?'

A loud sneeze from Goering interrupted his flow and drew Hitler's attention to the armed forces chief and founder of the Gestapo.

'You're too fat, Hermann,' Hitler said. 'Maybe we should use you as our secret weapon: make you centre forward and flatten the opposition? That would make victory certain.'

The others quickly joined in the joke, guffawing at Goering's expense.

'Well, if I were playing,' Goering snorted, 'I'd make absolutely certain we won.'

'Oh, and how would you do that?' asked Hitler, still smiling.

'Simple. I'd tell the Russians I'd shoot them if they won. A pity we didn't do that to the English in '38. I had to sit through the shame of it.'

They all darkly remembered the Germany–England football match at Berlin's Olympic Stadium before over a hundred thousand fans, all shouting for Germany: 'DEUTSCHLAND, DEUTSCHLAND, DEUTSCHLAND!'

But . . . inspired by Stanley Matthews, England had run rings round the Germans, and won 6–3.

'Yes, yes, we were badly prepared then,' grunted Hitler. 'It won't happen again. You are right. Just in case, tell the Russians they'll be strung up if they try too hard.'

Turning to Himmler and Goebbels, he said, 'I'm entrusting you both with arrangements. Herr Himmler— select the best professionals. Make sure the Kiev team is weak, root out all communists and Jews. Our boys won't play against rats and other vermin. And fill the stadium with local people to witness our victory. That'll break their spirit.

'You, Herr Goebbels, will invite the press and make sure the entire world hears the match on the wireless. That way, everyone will know the German nation cannot be beaten.'

Suddenly, he burst out laughing. It was like the crackle of dry leaves underfoot.

'*Ach, Todesspiel*, Match of Death . . . I like the sound of that!'

4

They came without warning.

It was a warm Sunday morning in late June, the eve of Midsummer's Day.

I was playing football. About a dozen of us had gone to the local park, put down shirts for goalposts in a clearing between the trees, and picked up sides.

All at once, we heard this buzzing, like angry bluebottles butting their heads against a window pane. At first, we thought we were in for an electric storm, one of those sudden summer showers that fall from clear skies and catch you on the hop.

We played on, at any moment expecting big splish-sploshes on our bare shoulders. So involved were we in the kick-about that we paid no more heed to the approaching thunderclaps.

Then, suddenly, dark shadows passed over the grass, as if giant eagles were blocking out the sun. Everyone looked up. And there in the clear blue sky was the strangest sight.

Wave upon wave of aeroplanes. Each wave contained about ten of the great brutes, flying in a sort of football formation. Five forwards, three half backs, two backs, and a goalie at the rear.

Naturally, we assumed they were ours: no one had told us *we* were at war with anybody.

A few of the lads waved their arms and hollered up to the gallant pilots. It was such an exciting mixture of sights and sounds, and it made us feel proud and safe. If war did come, it was good to know we had the Red Air Force to protect us.

When the planes had roared over, we went on with the game, relieved it hadn't been rained off by a summer storm.

We were not to know that the most terrible storm was about to break upon our heads.

A few minutes later, we heard this terrific bang—like someone bursting a paper bag in your ear. Then came loud explosions—bang, b-a-n-g, B A N G!—one after the other.

The ground shook beneath our feet and a fierce gust of wind ripped through the trees, almost bowling us over. Our goalpost shirts flew off like flitting ghosts towards the river; the leather ball followed, as if driven by some invisible piledriver.

For the first time we started to get the wind up. It was as much a sense of awe as of fear. What on earth was happening? Was the world coming to an end?

No one bothered about football any more. In any case our old leather ball had gone with the wind, blown into the river. We just stood there, rooted to the spot, staring towards the bangs.

'What the hell is it?' asked my best pal Makar, trying to control his shaky voice.

'Search me,' I mumbled.

'Seems to be coming from the airport,' Abram, our goalie, said, shielding his eyes from the sun.

'Maybe a plane's crashed,' suggested Yakov.

That must be it, for just then dusty clouds billowed up into the sky above the treetops. Swirling grey-brown smoke began to mingle with red flames and flying black debris.

As we stared wide-eyed towards the airport, we suddenly heard another sound—the one that had first interrupted our game. The drone of aeroplanes!

'They're coming back,' Makar yelled.

An awful thought struck me.

What if they *aren't* ours? What if the Germans had bombed the airport, destroying our planes? They wouldn't . . . would they? They couldn't . . . could they?

'Quick,' I shouted. 'Run for cover. Maybe they're *not* ours!'

We took to our heels as the planes roared low overhead. This time I looked up as I ran. And in the smoke-darkened sky I spotted black crosses on some of the planes. I'd never seen those crosses before: suddenly they looked evil, the mark of death, like iron crosses on a grave.

No one waved to the pilots this time. We were too desperate to get home, out of harm's way. Dad would know what was going on. He always explained mysteries to me: how birds fly, how fish breathe underwater, why there's no god, why Hitler wants war.

It was Dad who'd brought us to town when times were hard in the village and people were starving. He was a geography teacher, deputy head at School No. 37 on the Dnieper Embankment. Mum was a nurse at the district polyclinic.

As we dashed through the park and out on to the main street, the *Kreshchatik*, we realized that something really terrible had happened. So many people were milling round: women were wailing, children were blubbering, men were shouting and bawling.

No one seemed to know why!

To add to the hullabaloo, fire engines came clattering and hooting down the highway.

Above the din an eerie voice suddenly crackled to life over the city loudspeakers. The system was mostly used for holidays when happy, bright music and news poured out. We all listened hard, scarcely daring to breathe in case we missed a word.

'ATTENTION, CITIZENS, ATTENTION!'

17

The hubbub died down at once. In calm, grave tones the bass voice boomed out:

'At o-three-thirty today, the twenty second of June, Hitlerite Fascists treacherously invaded our country. *WE ARE AT WAR*. Stand by for further information.'

He repeated the message two or three times.

When the words had sunk in, the stunned crowds swiftly broke up as people rushed home for further news.

WAR!

What did it mean?

How would it affect football?

I'd just joined Dinamo Kiev Juniors and had a big game tomorrow, against Moscow Dinamo. Then, out of the gloom, came a ray of hope. A silly idea really. One that pops up when you're dead scared and don't know what's happening.

If *men* get called up, I might find myself playing for the Reserves, or even the first team—sooner than I'd dared hope.

There might be a silver lining in the war clouds, after all.

5

Next day, Monday, few people went to work. The entire city was a-buzz with rumour. Gossips had a field day.

The Germans had knocked out the entire Red Air Force by their surprise air-raids.

German troops could be expected at any moment.

The Fascists would kill men who refused to work for them and send women as slave workers to Germany— along with our cattle and grain. We would starve.

Stalin had fled Moscow for deepest Siberia.

The loudspeakers were silent.

People stared up at them, willing them to speak, desperately hoping for reassuring news. If only Stalin would speak to us. We trusted in him. But the wireless did give notice of an important government statement at midday.

'Oh, that's all right, then,' said Mum at breakfast. 'One word from Comrade Stalin and the Germans will scuttle off home.'

Dad, being a communist, was upset by Mum's tone.

'Natalia Petrovna,' he said sternly, 'this is no time for sarcasm. At this historic moment we need a strong leader. Who else can save us from Hitler?'

When angry, Dad always called her Natalia Petrovna, like a schoolboy addressing his teacher. Dad's parents were poor peasants who'd done well out of the new farm system, whereas Mum's had been well-off farmers who'd been arrested ten years before. We didn't know where they were now, even whether they were alive. I just remember waving goodbye when I was a toddler. Off they slithered on a sledge one snowy day with nothing but the clothes they sat in.

Mum had never forgiven Stalin. But she only sounded off behind closed doors. Much to Dad's embarrassment, she also kept a holy icon in the corner of the living room, and often said prayers before it. That morning, she'd lit a candle beneath Christ's wooden image.

It was Mum who'd given the girls their names: Vera—Faith, Nadia—Hope, and Lyuba—Love. Dad's only victory was to call me Vladimir, Vova for short, after Vladimir Lenin, the first Soviet leader. Mum had promised him Ninel—Lenin spelled backwards—if it had been a girl.

Now, Mum wasn't to be silenced.

'If Stalin hadn't shot our army leaders back in '37 and trusted in Hitler's promises, we'd be better prepared for war. Who knows, maybe the Germans will treat us better than Stalin: they are Christians at least!'

'Keep your voice down,' muttered Dad, 'or you'll get us all shot. At least listen to what Comrade Stalin has to say.'

'I hope Uncle Stalin is on time,' I piped up. 'I've got to be at the stadium at one thirty. Today's my big day.'

My three sisters were more excited for their soon-to-be-famous brother than were Mum and Dad. Vera, who was a year older than me, had appointed herself my personal coach.

'Remember,' she said: 'keep your eye on the ball, head down when you shoot, and meet the ball cleanly when you head for goal.'

She tapped her freckled brow below the centre parting, her two long plaits bobbing against her back with the effort.

The ten-year-old twins, Nadia and Lyuba, clapped their hands in anticipation of the football treat. The whole

20

Grechko family had planned to come to watch me. Mum, however, was about to pour icy water on my Big Day.

'Vova, now don't be upset. Your dad and I won't be going. There's a war on, after all. What if the Germans arrive while we're all out? Anyway, your dad's likely to become some big shot political commissar. And I've got our relatives in the country to worry about.'

Dad gave her a sour look, but he had to agree.

'Sorry, son. Your mum's right on one thing: peacetime's over. We're at war now.'

'Does that mean no more school?' exclaimed Nadia excitedly.

Vera scolded her.

'*Durochka!* You don't want to end up a milkmaid, do you? If school's shut down I'll teach you myself.'

Naturally, I felt let down by Mum and Dad. To me football came first, war second. Anyway, it was hard to imagine war. Yet when I remembered those droning planes, I realized one thing: war spelled D-E-A-T-H, that's for sure.

I sighed. If Dad went off to the army, I'd be left at home, the only male in the house, bossed about by four females. Since our flat had only two rooms, there was nowhere to hide. Mum and Dad slept on the living room settee, while we kids had the bedroom: the three girls in the bed, me on the floor. With Dad away, maybe I'd have the settee all to myself, with Mum and sisters in the bedroom.

War might not be *all* bad.

Like all Soviet citizens, midday found us crowded round the wireless set. After a long wait broken only by loud crackling, a sombre voice spoke to us.

It wasn't Stalin. It was Molotov, the 'Hammer' as he was called. Stalin was 'Man of Steel', Molotov—the 'Hammer'. We listened open-mouthed.

'Citizens, we are at war. Yesterday at four o'clock in the morning, German troops invaded our country without warning or declaration of war.

'This is a Great Patriotic War. We are fighting for our lives . . . We now call on every patriot—every man, woman, and child—to rise up and defend their homes. And if the foe advances into our homeland, we will attack him on every side, from forest and hill, from bunker and cellar—just as our ancestors did in defeating Napoleon.

'Forward, comrades, to victory. Our cause is just, the enemy will be destroyed, victory will be ours!'

For a full minute we sat silent, waiting for further news. Was that it? But the terrible words were followed only by the national anthem, 'The Internationale', and patriotic music.

Why hadn't Stalin spoken? Where was he? Was he still alive?

I was the first to break the silence.

'Right, then,' I said. 'First we'll beat Moscow Dinamo, then the Germans.'

6

The boneshaker tram ride to the stadium that Monday afternoon was eerie. Never had I seen such hustle and bustle on the streets.

Soldiers were stacking sandbags against walls and doors, daubing signs, pouring pails of water into tanks, erecting shelters. The men all looked so young and green, real rosy-cheeked peasant lads. How would they fare in battle? Against battle-hardened Germans who'd already had two years of war, and had swept across the whole of Europe?

Women were staggering along, weighed down by bags bursting with rye loaves and potatoes, as much as they could lay their hands on.

Men were boarding up shops, taking down give-away signs—like Militia Station, *Agitpunkt*, Communist Party HQ.

Many were just standing idly on street corners in knots of six or seven, waving their arms, shrugging shoulders, wondering what would happen next.

A few families had packed their belongings · on handcarts which they were pushing through the streets. Goodness knows where they were going. In the Tanks versus Carts race, there could be only one winner.

Anyway, the loudspeakers had warned that people caught fleeing the city would be shot on the spot. Surely the fugitives wouldn't risk being killed before the shooting started in earnest?

When I climbed the hill to the stadium just before one thirty, I half expected to find the gates padlocked. But, no,

23

they were wide open, with no one to stop fans—or Germans for that matter—from pouring in. I made my way to the changing rooms beneath the main stand and breathed a sigh of relief.

Everything seemed normal. The sweet smell of muscle rub, the clatter of studs on concrete, the babble of over-excited voices, the grunts from the masseur's bench as Old Basher pummelled his victims into putty.

Coach met me at the changing room door, a worried frown on his lined face.

'Good lad, Grechko,' he grunted. 'I knew I could count on you.'

'Is the match definitely on?' I asked.

'Of course,' he replied, as if it was a stupid question. 'As long as we can put out a team, football carries on as per usual. We're just a couple of players short at the moment. No sign of the bloomin' ref either.'

He glanced anxiously down the corridor. I'd passed the Visitors' Changing Room on my way and knew our opponents were already stripping off. They'd travelled overnight by train. No one had warned them about a one-way ticket to hell. I wondered how they'd be getting back home.

At two o'clock, our Kiev Dinamo junior team ran out for a pre-match warm up. An hour to go before kick-off. Coach reckoned we youngsters needed a 'feel' of the stadium and pitch before the match started. For two or three of us this was our first match in the giant stadium, and we naturally felt jittery.

The entry of the gladiators wasn't exactly met by a thunderous roar. Yet there was a fair sprinkling of young fans on wooden benches behind the goals. I spotted my sisters at once by the blue ribbons in their fair hair; they were sitting together high up on the south terrace. I waved an arm in salute, like a star greeting his public.

The Moscow team had already occupied the right-hand goalmouth and were kicking in, sprinting, jumping, stretching their muscles.

Gosh, they did look hefty. What did they feed Moscow kids on? *Hercules* porridge by the look of it!

Coach liked Order. Not everyone banging balls at Abram Gorinstein, our goalie. So he had his centre forward—me—shooting at goal, while the rest formed circles out on the flanks, loosening up, passing, heading, keeping busy. No one stood around waiting for the ball. As it was, we only had two patchy leather balls, including the match ball!

By two thirty we couldn't wait to get started. Still no sign of the ref or two linesmen; nor our two missing players. In the end, we had to 'borrow' a couple of Moscow boys; our coach refereed, while their coach and 'sponge man' ran the lines. It was only a friendly, after all.

What a thrill it was to run out from the dark tunnel into the sunshine of our Dinamo Kiev Stadium. It had been built ten years after the Revolution, in 1927, and was one of the world's greatest, seating some seventy thousand fans.

It didn't matter that only a few hundred were there to cheer us on. We were 'their' team, in the familiar white shirts with black collars and the 'D' diamond on our chests; we had black shorts and socks. Our opponents had changed from Dinamo white to red away shirts and white shorts.

Coach blew his whistle and I kicked off.

It was my first touch of the ball. And my last!

For just as I tapped the ball to our inside right, we heard the strangest sound. Although we didn't know it then, this was the air-raid siren.

Neee-awww, Neee-awww, Neee-awww!

It scared the living daylights out of us.

We all stood stock still, staring up at the sky. But, apart from a flock of startled pigeons, the heavens were clear. All that marred the blue canopy was a bright orange sun right above us.

A nearby loudspeaker spluttered into life.

'Testing, testing . . . This is air-raid warning practice. Proceed at once to your nearest shelter. This is air-raid practice. In twenty minutes you will hear the all-clear.'

Coach blew his whistle and picked up the ball.

'Back to the changing rooms, lads. We'll re-start at three thirty.'

Instead of making a dash for the changing room, I ran over to my sisters. Fans were already hurrying out, ushered to the nearest public shelter by militia women.

'Re-start in half an hour,' I yelled. 'Get to the shelter.'

They waved to show they'd heard.

But we never did re-start the match. No sooner had the all-clear sounded and people had begun to emerge from their hiding places, chatting cheerily, than it started all over again, and we trooped back below.

Coach kept glaring at his stopwatch, clicking his tongue impatiently and stamping his studs on the concrete floor.

'Typical cock-up,' he kept muttering. 'Couldn't organize a piss-up in a vodka factory. How will we win the war with such sloppiness?'

We smiled. No one could accuse Ivan Ivanovich of being an enemy of the people. He'd fought in World War I, and then for the Red Guards in our Civil War. Now he was Political Commissar at the Club *and* an officer in the NKVD. No stauncher patriot than he.

The minutes dragged by—ten, twenty, thirty. Just as we were beginning to think we'd missed the all-clear, we heard it . . .

26

That same sinister hummm-hummm-hummm we'd heard the day before.

They were coming back!

7

It had to be them.

In our concrete bunker we could hear but not see. A bare dusty bulb cast a ghostly shadow on the young faces, making them look old and sallow. Only the eyes, bright and curious, remained young. Like tiny lanterns in the gloom, their light flickered from door to ceiling, from face to face, searching for an answer.

Why *us*? What have *we* done to them?

We only want to play football. If they want a fight, let's settle it on the football pitch.

But *they* couldn't hear us. *They* didn't care about football. *They* had other things on their mind—like bombing us to bits and ruling the world.

Coach did his best to keep us calm. He was the only one who'd seen bombs, shells, warplanes before. He'd also seen innocent victims—thousands upon thousands of them; war-mangled bodies of men, women, and children.

That was then, twenty-five years ago, in the war to end all wars. Now it was starting all over again.

'Listen, lads, I'll be blunt. You know me. The way I see it is like this. Hitler always intended to attack us, to destroy communism, his biggest hate. Stalin knew that. Both played for time. *They* wanted to conquer the west first. *We* needed to make more guns and tanks, shore up our defences.'

He sighed and searched our faces.

'If Hitler pits his armies against us, we won't hold out for long; we'll have to give way—two steps backward, three steps forward later on. Our raw *muzhiks* can't stop the Fascists.

28

'But our three generals will: General Winter, General Mud, and General People. Our people will win through in the end. They'll sacrifice everything to protect their homeland.

'It'll take time, maybe two or three years; and millions of young people like you won't live to love and grow old. But for their sakes, we'll triumph in the end.'

We smiled bravely at his words, though he could see we weren't convinced.

'Look,' he said, 'it's like a game of football. If you're up against a strong opponent, you give ground, soak up the pressure. Then, when he's tired himself out, overstretched himself—wham!—you hit him on the break. Tactics, comrades, that's what wins matches—and wars.'

As he finished speaking, thunder erupted. Not in the skies, down here on earth. Somewhere outside, nearby. At once Coach stood up and went next door to talk to the Moscow team. Meantime, we huddled together, comforted by the closeness of warm, sweaty, skinny bodies.

I kept worrying about my sisters. Hopefully, they were safe, deep underground in the newly-built Metro. 'Sport' Station was close by the football ground. In any case, we were a good half-hour from the city centre—if that's where it was raining bombs.

But what about Mum and Dad? Would they be down in the basement of our new ten-storey block of flats? What if the whole lot toppled down on them?

My thoughts were shattered by a terrific explosion. It made the floor heave and walls shake; plaster showered down on us like falling snow, and the lamp went out.

Surely they wouldn't bomb our brand new stadium, the spoilsports! Didn't Fascists play football? There must be a Convention or something against bombing football grounds, like Red Cross ambulances and hospitals.

As Coach returned, the swaying bulb suddenly came back on.

'And God said "Let there be light!"' he said, snapping his fingers and smiling grimly.

We couldn't help laughing. His head and shoulders were white from falling whitewash plaster. But our footballing god had no more miracles up his sleeve. He just sat gloomily silent, staring up at the flaky ceiling, waiting, waiting . . .

The bombing lasted just over an hour. In the lull that followed we couldn't wait to escape from our tomb. Yet Coach kept us back, saying it wasn't safe yet. To distract us he told stories of the Civil War, of the legendary commander Chapayev, of young Anya and Petya who'd died for the cause, of the first Soviet leader Vladimir Lenin.

Anything to take our minds off what awaited us above ground. Only when the wail of the all-clear reached us did he crank himself up on his creaky legs.

'Right, lads,' he said, 'after me, single file, quick march.'

We followed him out of the changing room; as we waited in the dingy corridor, he gave instructions to the lads next door. Both teams lined up, shoulder to shoulder, as if going out to play a game of football.

We trotted along in pairs behind the two coaches, down the dusty whitewashed passage, up the dark tunnel and on to the green pitch. We were still in shirts and shorts, though no one gave a thought to playing football.

We had no idea what we'd find at the end of the tunnel. Even so, *no one* expected the sight that greeted us.

Day had turned to night. A purplish black smokescreen covered sun and sky.

Hundreds of fires were spewing dense smoke into the air, forming a giant mushroom cloud above the town—the once-beautiful 'Mother of all Russian cities', with its gold onion domes on stately churches, its green hills on one side and broad blue Dnieper River on the other.

Now gold-green-blue had turned to muddy black.

The stadium stood on a hill above the city, so we could see for miles beneath the swirling, choking smoke. Apart from charred debris and ash falling from the skies, the stadium seemed unharmed. Even the goalposts and corner flags stood like sentinels, defiantly erect.

A scruffy black and white dog was running round the pitch, sniffing the grass and yelping in lonely fear. The moment we appeared, it came bounding over to us, licking our hands and whining with relief at finding human company.

The city burned. Since most houses were of wood, it didn't take much to set off a raging bonfire—just a hundred or so fire bombs. I hoped Mum and Dad were safe in their stone fortress. But what about Vera and the twins?

I appealed to Coach.

'Ivan Ivanovich, my sisters came to the match; they must be sheltering nearby, probably in the Metro. Is it all right to go and see?'

'Hold your horses, Vova,' was all he said.

Having sized up the situation, he turned to address players and officials. In a stern voice, he shouted, 'As Political Commissar at this Stadium, I am taking charge. At least until the city defence command sorts itself out.

'Now, look, this is what we'll do. We're a fit sports unit used to working as a team. That's a big asset in wartime. First we'll see who needs help, OK? Keep together. We'll start at the Metro. Let's go.'

He marched stiffly off through the main gates in the direction of 'Sport' Station. We must have looked a weird sight in our football boots, shirts, and shorts, trailing behind a limping, grey-haired man in a worn tracksuit. But, then, nothing was normal that fateful afternoon.

Our world had been sent cartwheeling out of control, head over heels, topsy-turvy; and it had landed with a CRASH and a BANG in a tangled heap.

Nothing and no one would ever be the same again.

8

The explosion that showered our heads with white flakes had come from Revolution Square beside the Metro Station. We could smell it before we could see it. Like coarse black *mahorka* tobacco.

As we drew near, we saw trams on fire, twisted rails rearing up like crazy horses, jagged glass splinters glinting in the firelight, and a deep pudding-basin hole in the ground.

By a miracle the bomb had missed the station building by a whisker and landed in the square. The only victim was poor old Lenin who'd lost his granite head.

All the same, the blast had set light to the station's wooden doors and rubber door jambs. They were well ablaze by the time we arrived, blocking any escape from inside or rescue attempt from outside. Through the black smoke and red-orange flames we could plainly see the terror-stricken faces of those trapped in the entry hall. Most were youngsters who had come to the match.

Many were screaming for help, holding out begging arms, some bent double, choking on the thick black smoke. Never had I felt so scared and helpless. The two tracksuited men tried to reach the doors of the burning building; but the fierce heat and grasping flames drove them back. It looked as if those inside were doomed: they couldn't get out, we couldn't get in.

Turning back to us, Coach yelled, 'Quick, tear up saplings, bring fallen branches, anything to beat out the fire. Fetch damp earth to smother the flames. Fast as you can before the whole lot goes up in smoke. If we don't reach them soon, the poor devils'll roast in Hell.'

We hardly needed urging. Most of our team had relatives trapped inside.

From the little park behind the square we pulled and dug up whatever we could with our bare hands. We also grabbed the row of earth buckets outside the Metro. Then we set up a relay chain, each link passing on branches and pails of earth until they reached the firefighters.

Coach sent a few lads down to the river; they soon came racing back with old tin cans and buckets, splashing their contents along the way. The muddy water went sizzling into the blaze.

The heat was so intense we all had to take short bursts in the front line. When I took my turn before the roaring furnace, I worked in a frenzy, beating at the fire with leafy branches, pelting it with buckets of moist earth, flinging on water, cursing the flames: 'Take that, you swine! You son-of-a-bitch! You Fascist pig!'—until the heat drove me back.

Quick intake of air, hold breath, dart in, throw, curse, jump back double quick.

The inferno seemed to be gratefully gulping down all we threw at it, and bellowing out for more like some insatiable fire-breathing dragon.

Above the fire's roar, all at once I heard a shout. It was both familiar and strange. 'Vova, Vova!'

Through the billowing purple veil I saw Vera's blackened face, wide-eyed with fear.

'Help! Save us!'

'Hold on, Sis,' I yelled.

'Hurry, Vova, hurry!'

Her cries faded into a rasping fit of coughing.

The danger was painfully obvious. They were trapped in the smoke-filled entrance hall; the flames were flicking out fiery tongues from both the oak doors in front and the wooden escalators behind. Even more deadly was the thick black smoke swirling up from burning rubber.

It was touch and go whether we or the fire would reach them first. The smoke and fire were winning.

I redoubled my efforts, unaware of my hair smouldering and hands blistering. The heat and smoke were overpowering. I could scarcely catch my breath. It felt as if boiling oil was being forced down my throat into my lungs. Nevertheless, I battled on, gasping and wheezing.

I was vaguely aware of dribbles of people joining the rescue team. They were lugging buckets of sand, soil, and water. With our combined efforts, the tide was slowly, slowly turning. Under Coach's orders, we were now concentrating on the weakest link in the chain of fire—a single end door.

Soon a small space appeared; though flames clung stubbornly to the frame, they no longer had the power to leap across the gap left by a broken pane of glass.

'Coach,' I cried. 'I'm small enough to squeeze through. Let me go in and bring out the injured. Every second helps. Some must be choking to death.'

A look of uncertainty swept over his sooty face, as if he couldn't risk his star striker. But he finally nodded gravely.

'Go on, then, Vova. For Christ's sake, watch yourself.'

I took a deep gulp of air, held a wet rag over my mouth and took a running jump through the burning doorframe.

I made it safely—apart from singed hair and eyebrows. I was now in—but would I get out? There was only one way to find out.

A quick glance round told me there were sixty or seventy people in the smoky hall, most about my age— thirteen to fifteen year olds. They had come to watch a game of football on a quiet sunny afternoon in June . . .

Most were choking, wheezing, trying to catch their breath; some were on hands and knees, head bent, searching for a draught of air. A few were sprawled on the floor, quite still, their faces black, their features twisted in agony.

For a brief moment, I wondered where the rest were. Hundreds must be still trapped underground, on the platforms. But right now I was surrounded by screaming bodies. At my sudden appearance faint hope flickered in their terrified eyes. Vera was at my side, gasping, spluttering, yet taking over.

'Not a . . . mo-ment too soon,' she said through choking coughs. 'We'll c-c-carry the worst . . . out.'

Even facing death, Vera had to be in charge!

We lifted up a senseless child and rushed with him through the burning doorframe.

The firefighters raised a cheer, and two elderly women at once took care of the squirming bundle. The fresh air seemed to revive the boy at once; that gave us hope. Had she not collapsed, coughing, in the road, Vera would have returned with me.

I took another deep breath and dashed back again, feeling like a circus dog jumping through a burning hoop. Two other lads joined me and we soon had ten of the worst victims out; by this time some of those trapped had plucked up courage to follow our example and leap through the flames to safety.

Soon everyone in the hallway had been brought out. The flames were smothered and we were just preparing to tackle the escalator fire when two fire engines arrived, followed by several ambulances.

Coach handed over command and we were able to take a breather.

Not all the little black bundles we'd brought out showed signs of life; but they were quickly stretchered out of sight into the waiting ambulances and taken off somewhere or other. Were any hospitals left standing after the raid? Perhaps the dead and injured would be taken to medical posts out of town?

I sank down on the grass verge with Vera. My two younger sisters, Nadia and Lyuba, had been driven off for treatment—smoke had clogged their lungs. Only then did I realize how tired I was. And the pain! My face, hands, and legs had turned into a mottled mass of flaming red weals and white scaly blisters. Never had I suffered such agony in all my fifteen years.

Vera did her best. Ignoring her own wounds, she tore strips off her blouse and wrapped them round my bare arms and legs. There wasn't much she could do about my face.

'A real Hero of Labour,' she said in genuine admiration. 'Didn't know you had it in you. Must save those precious legs for scoring goals . . . '

She rambled on, trying to take my mind off the burns. It was more her looks than her words that helped. I couldn't help smiling at her panda face. Apart from pale eyes and teeth, the rest of her was sooty black.

'You look like a poor colonial slave,' I muttered.

'And you're a chicken plucked and singed for the pot,' she retorted.

After she'd bandaged me up, we sat in silence, staring down at the burning city. The stray mongrel from the stadium silently joined us, squatting at my side and looking mournfully at the blaze.

'Mum and Dad are somewhere down there in the rubble,' said Vera quietly.

9

By rights I ought to have had my burns treated in hospital. But I hardly needed the sighs of nurses to tell me they had far worse cases on their hands. It was Coach who led me off to the stadium cuts and bruises room. Even Vera didn't dare meddle with Ivan Ivanovich.

I wasn't the only 'wounded soldier'; almost everyone had weals and blisters. Most of us were coughing up black gritty phlegm; Coach had lost what remained of his hair, and his tracksuit had more holes than a goal net. We footballers looked just as sorry a sight as those we'd rescued.

Once we'd had a bath—in cold water!—and been patched up by Old Basher, who moaned about us using up his year's supply of bandages, lint, and iodine, we all gathered in the canteen.

It was about six o'clock, and Coach had glasses of hot black tea and sweet wafer biscuits ready for everyone.

Our number had grown to thirty-three—the two teams and officials, five girls, including Vera, and the black and white stray who ate more biscuits than the rest of us. He, like us, perked up after the food and hot tea.

Since the dog had adopted me as his new master, I gave him a name: 'Dinamo', 'dee-nah-mo'—'power in motion', as I'd heard somewhere. It suited him as much as calling a giant 'Tiny'.

Coach shuffled to the serving counter, leaning crookedly against it. We sat round him at the wooden tables. By now Ivan Ivanovich had swapped his tattered tracksuit for a pair of old baggy blue shorts and a white shirt that barely went round his midriff.

'Heroes, the lot of you,' he began. 'You saved many young lives today. Our Moscow comrades merit special praise. We're grateful, brothers.' He nodded to them. 'As for you Kievans, I know you're worrying about friends and relatives in the city . . . '

'Why don't we phone for news?' asked one lad.

'Phones are down,' muttered Coach.

'Can't the militia help?'

'It's bedlam, son. There's one helluvalot of casualties, I'm afraid.'

'We can't just sit here awaiting orders,' grumbled the Moscow coach.

'No, you're right, brother,' said Coach. 'I tell you what. Let's form three units. We'll go in search of our families, help where we can, and report back at around ten o'clock. Right?'

It was as good a plan as any. Since it was Midsummer's Day we had plenty of daylight to work with.

We formed groups according to districts. My unit consisted of five Kiev players, Vera, me, and four Moscow lads. Although the Moscow coach was in charge, I acted as guide since he wasn't familiar with the city.

No one had any idea how we were to get into town. No public transport was running; in any case, most streets were probably blocked by rubble and collapsing walls. None of us walking wounded fancied the painful three-mile slog to our homes, but we had no choice.

We will never forget that evening; it's seared forever on our minds like a red-hot branding iron on a calf's rump.

After half a mile we began to see the scale of the tragedy. A peaceful old city had become a battlefield of smoking rubble. If wooden, the houses had gone up in flames; if concrete, they had collapsed like a pack of cards.

A twenty-storey apartment block reduced to a four-metre mound of smoking, broken stones.

Not a single pane of glass remained intact—great shop windows smashed to smithereens, like greeny-blue ice fragments littering pavement and road.

And it was so eerily quiet. Where were all the people? Were they still in the basements? If so, it didn't bear thinking about . . . They must now be gasping their last breath in sealed tombs.

'Shouldn't we stop and try to dig them out?' asked one lad.

'What good would *that* do?' the Moscow leader replied gruffly. 'We can't rescue them with our bare hands. Our mission is clear: families first. War has made us all soldiers, and the first thing a soldier learns is to carry out orders.'

He was right, of course. Even if we had saved two or three, there were hundreds, maybe thousands, buried in the rubble.

We walked on, now and then having to clamber over barriers of twisted timbers, trees, lorries, and fallen masonry. The closer we came to the city centre, the more signs of life appeared: medical orderlies in once-white coats carrying dusty bundles on stretchers; soldiers and militia digging in the rubble; whole families squatting by the roadside, crying from fear and confusion.

Others people's tragedies partly took my mind off my own woes. I had never known such pain. I remember once burning my thumb on a bonfire. Boy, did it hurt. But that was nothing to what I now suffered, *all over my body*. It was agony. Only the thought of finding Mum and Dad alive kept me going.

Then there was Vera. We were lagging behind the others because Vera kept having to stop, fighting to catch her breath and spitting up great black globules of liquid soot.

When we finally arrived at Taras Shevchenko Prospect, I called out, 'Hold on, Fyodor Abramovich.'

When we caught up, I made a suggestion.

'To save time, we could split up, each go our separate ways and report back in a couple of hours.'

'Make it an hour and a half,' he said. 'And if anyone needs a hand, you know where to find us. We'll do what we can to help out here.'

He knew our search was a personal affair. What he also knew, but kept to himself, was that we weren't likely to find anyone alive. By ourselves we could grieve privately.

Leaving the Moscow crew on Shevchenko Square, now lacking its big statue of our national poet Taras, Vera and I set off down a no-longer-familiar street.

Gone was the *Bulochnaya* with its sour-sweet smell of fresh bread and rolls.

Gone was the *Molochnaya* with its curds, creamy buttermilk, sour cream, and cheeses.

Gone was the *Apteka* where Mum had got her steel-rimmed specs and Dad his mustard plasters.

Only one corner of the *Kniga* store remained, spilling its dusty red volumes of Lenin and Stalin into the street.

Lenin lives! I thought, repeating a phrase drummed into us at school.

Once we reached the corner, we'd be on our quiet, poplar-lined avenue of neat, ten-storey apartment blocks. We quickened our step, hearts beating fast.

At the end of the main street, our hopes rose—there was little sign of damage here. Maybe the bombs hadn't reached this far?

It was Vera who turned the corner first. I saw her suddenly stop, put her hand to her mouth, and collapse in a fit of coughing. I thought it was her lungs. As I reached her I saw that our street had escaped with barely a scratch. What a relief. Yet as I followed Vera's shaking hand, I saw a single gap in the line of ten white tower blocks. It was like a set of teeth with one tooth missing.

A single block of flats must have taken a direct hit, while the others had escaped untouched.

That's fate for you: being in the wrong place at the wrong time.

'Oh, Mum,' groaned Vera, putting her hands over her eyes and sobbing.

Only then did I realize.

It was our block that was the missing tooth!

I should have cried my eyes out. Yet I couldn't. The flames of war had seared my mind and body with so much pain that I could take no more. I was all burnt out. Never seeing Mum and Dad again should have cut me to the quick. But war had drained me of emotion.

I stood and stared, then turned away.

'Right, let's get on,' I said. 'We've a lot to do.'

10

Adolf Hitler rubbed his hands and permitted himself a hint of a smile. Like a glimmer of pale sunshine between scowling storm clouds.

'Our invasion of Russia has made the whole world hold its breath,' Goebbels was saying, spreading his arms to embrace the globe.

'The world should thank us,' snarled Hitler. 'For ridding it of communists and Jews, the enemies of European civilization. They are *vermin*. Our mission is to clear the way for the Master Race. Russia will be our India, the Slavs our slaves!'

He paused to let his words sink in, like blotting paper swallowing ink. Goering quickly grabbed the opportunity to butt in.

'May I report, *mein Führer*? Operation Red Beard, Barbarossa, is a total success. On 22 June we sent in seven infantry regiments spearheaded by four Panzer groups of 3,750 tanks—over three million men in all, seventy per cent of *Wehrmacht* strength.

'Our Romanian and Hungarian allies support our southern flank, the Finns our northern. We also have several thousand Ukrainian nationalists fighting with us; they hate Jews and Bolsheviks as much as we do.

'On Day One, two thousand Luftwaffe planes destroyed one thousand two hundred Red planes, mostly on the ground. Within three weeks we wiped out six thousand

43

planes and three thousand five hundred tanks, killed a million of the enemy and took a million prisoners.

'Our armies have covered thirty to forty kilometres a day, and are now closing in on Kiev and Leningrad; we will shortly be at the gates of Moscow. General Guderian's Panzers have smashed through the Red Army front like a steel fist through a crumbling mud wall. Stalin is paralysed with fear. The war will be over before winter.'

Hitler was not content.

'I want Kiev captured and destroyed. The German people must have the city as their prize. Crush it like a nut in a nutcracker. Spare no one: man, woman, or child. Take no prisoners: we won't waste food that could feed Germans.'

Field Marshall Goering knew what Kiev meant to Hitler, and he said nothing. But his doubts gnawed away at him. What if they wasted precious months in fighting for Kiev? Winter could set in by the time they stormed Moscow. That would give Stalin time to shore up his defences.

But he held his tongue.

28 July Moscow

Stalin was a mere bag of bones in a grey tunic. He had been working round the clock, trusting no one but himself.

When he had finally forced the truth out of his commanders a month back, five days after the attack, he admitted how wrong he had been—but only to himself. He had ignored all warnings of a German invasion, refused to put troops on the alert.

Now, twenty million Soviet citizens were trapped, millions were dead, wounded, or taken prisoner.

It was too much for the 'Man of Steel'. He had fled to his country cottage, buried his head in the sand like an ostrich. For four long days. Only when colleagues had begged him to return—for the nation's sake—did he pull himself together and go back.

If he didn't stand and fight, who would? People trusted him, feared him, looked to him for leadership. They would follow him to Hell and back. He *had* to show a lead.

For the first time since the war began, he had addressed the nation by radio on 3rd July. He had called them his *Brothers and Sisters*, his *Friends*. His tone was sombre, but firm.

'Brothers and Sisters, Friends! This is no ordinary war. It is a War for the Fatherland. It is a fight to the death with Russia's deadliest foe. He must be left not a single engine, not a single wagon, not a single ear of grain or drop of fuel.

'This is *total* war, a war of the entire Soviet people. It is a choice between Soviet freedom or German slavery!'

Seven days later he had made himself Supreme Commander of the Red Army.

But he remained pig-headed, refusing to listen to wiser counsels. When Chief of Staff, Georgi Zhukov, advised him to abandon Kiev to the Germans—to save the armies of the south-west front—he dug his heels in. Instead of listening, he issued an order:

Ni shagu nazad!

'Not a step back! Every position, every patch of land must be defended to the last drop of blood!'

Zhukov resigned in a helpless rage.

Zhitomir fell on 10 July; it was only ten miles from Kiev. Smolensk fell on 16 July.

The Germans were closing in.

11

After discovering that we had no home—and probably no parents—Vera and I spent all our waking time helping out. So did the rest of the team. No time to mope or mourn.

There were sandbags to fill, windows to board up, scrap metal to collect, the dead and wounded to bring out and cart off to the cemetery. If we were children one day, we were seasoned veterans the next, comforting dying men and women. The worst was laying out the dead, row upon row, women and children on one side, men on the other.

Our spirit was growing hard too. If, or rather when, the Germans came we would sell our lives dearly.

A poem that went the rounds expressed the general feeling:

> If you don't want to give away
> All that you call your country,
> Then kill a German, kill a German,
> Every time you see one.

We hadn't seen one yet, but when we did . . .

Vera and I now lived at the Stadium; there was nowhere else to go. We slept on the wooden boards of the canteen floor: one side Kiev, the other Moscow. Coach and the other grown-ups dossed down in the changing rooms, on concrete floors.

We grandly called our resistance gang the International Brigade: Ukrainians and Russians together. We weren't sure what nationality our dog Dinamo was; he looked rather like a wild Cossack. The dog slept between Vera and

46

me, unsure whom to claim as master or mistress, and he followed us everywhere. He was better than any human at sniffing out survivors in the bombed buildings.

One of our first tasks was to dig for victims buried in the rubble. And since enemy planes flew over every night, dropping their deadly loads, *rubble* was all that was left in many parts of the city. Within a few weeks, it seemed that all the houses had sunk into the ground with burial mounds of brick heaped over them.

At least our sisters were safe. After three weeks, in mid-July, they were sent with our Moscow football friends on the last train out of Kiev. It saved their lives. Shortly after, even that escape route was blocked. It was too dangerous for trains to run the gauntlet of enemy bombs. In any case, burned-out trains and cattle wagons cluttered up the line to the south. And to the north-east the Germans had cut the Kiev–Moscow railway line at Shostka. The iron ring round Kiev was closing!

One day in late July, Coach came into the canteen with a stubby fellow in a simple army uniform and floppy riding boots.

'This is Comrade Nikita Khrushchov,' Coach announced with a flourish. 'He is Commissar to General Kirponos, Commander-in-Chief of the South-Western Front; *and* he is a personal confidant of Comrade Stalin.'

Coach always referred to fellow communists simply as 'Comrade', as if they were all equal, no higher than him.

At first, a few of us had sniggered at the name Kirponos—'Brick Nose'; but the mention of someone close to Stalin soon quietened us. Big Boots was a Big Cheese.

'Comrades and friends,' said the Commissar in Russian, 'I won't beat about the bush. We need volunteers at our Headquarters in Brovar, ten miles north-east of Kiev. We urgently need young boys and girls as scouts and medical orderlies.

'A word of warning. The work is dangerous, *very* dangerous; we cannot guarantee your safety. But . . . your country needs you as never before.'

Danger made it sound exciting and grown-up. Perhaps we could get to taking pot-shots at Germans.

We all volunteered. I volunteered on behalf of Dinamo.

Next morning early, as the dawn mists were still rising with the sun, we began our trek, led by the short, chubby Commissar in floppy boots. He took us along the dusty road out of Kiev, as if we were a company of new army recruits—left–right, left–right, left–right. Even Dinamo tried to keep in step.

The outlying villages of wooden huts with their goats and geese steadily gave way to rolling steppe of feather grass and, here and there, fields of yellow sunflowers, soya beans, and uncut corn. The evacuation of factory machines to the east took top priority. What with farmers being called up, there were only old women left to tend the fields. The harvest now lay ripe and bursting with golden ears of wheat and rye.

How would people eat if no one brought in the corn? Or perhaps Army Command already knew the Germans would come and take the harvest for themselves?

We stopped to rest at a largish village about midday. The Commissar took us directly to the Village Council, a tall wooden structure standing in the village centre— where the church had once been. The spire and onion domes may have gone, but there was no hiding the graves behind, with their crooked iron crosses.

Nailed to the door was a war poster bearing the words 'MOTHERLAND CALLS!' It showed a grave-faced woman in a red dress, her dark hair streaming. She was holding up the Military Oath in her left hand; behind her was a defiant barrier of bayonets.

Village women fussed about us, bringing out jars of pickled apples, cucumbers, and tomatoes, and peppering us with questions—as if we townsfolk had all the answers.

'Have you news of my son, Oles?'

'When will the war end?'

'Will the Germans come? Are they Christians?'

I wasn't sure what 'Christians' had to do with it, but we did our best to calm their fears by lying about the war.

As we left the village, they made the sign of the cross over us, begging us to send word to their men at the front.

We trudged on, reaching Brovar at about five o'clock. On the edge of the little town was a camp, Headquarters of the South-West Army. It was hard to tell what it was from a distance. The tents blended in with the trees and shrubs, and the anti-aircraft guns that ringed the base were camouflaged with silver-barked birch trees.

We marched through the centre of the camp, passing soldiers who stared wearily and glumly at us. Some were grizzled old-timers, others scarcely old enough to shave. To one side stood a group of Cossacks in their tall grey hats, proudly apart, feeding their horses.

I wondered what good horses would be against German tanks.

For the first time I began to feel helpless. How could horses, boys, and old men defeat the German army? Would the pious old women in the villages greet the Germans as fellow Christians who'd rid them of the godless communists? How would a country so divided come together?

Outside a small low hut set apart from the tents, we were told to await further orders. Some twenty minutes later, the Commissar returned to lead us down narrow wooden steps. The underground bunker was surprisingly spacious, with tunnels leading off into further rooms. It was rigged out with hurricane lamps, a field telephone, a dull metal samovar, tin plates, even an old bike in one corner.

At the trestle table, a brown satchel and large dusty map before him, sat a wiry, straight-backed figure with close-cropped hair and a roll-up in his mouth held by thin lips. Despite the muggy atmosphere, the officer had a sheepskin coat thrown over his shoulders.

My eye was caught by a red star on gold ribbons upon his chest—Hero of the Soviet Union! I'd never seen a real live hero before. I wondered how many Germans you had to kill to earn such a medal.

He paid no attention to our team of twelve boys, three girls, and a dog. We stood there awkwardly. As in church, I didn't know what to do with my hands: fold them in front or behind my back.

Suddenly, he jerked his head up and stared at us with bloodshot eyes. A weary smile creased his face as he flicked the cigarette from one corner of his mouth to the other.

'Ah, Dinamo Kiev FC,' he said. 'With mascot.'

That put us at ease. Obviously he was a football fan.

'I'm a Red Army Club supporter myself,' he said with a friendly grin. 'Still, to each his own.'

Then, growing serious, he leaned forward and said quietly, 'Listen, kids, we need your help. To slip a few passes through the German defence, score some winning goals. OK? Comrade Khrushchov will assign you to your duties. Best of luck, *Deenamovtsee!*'

His cheery last words at once faded away and a worried frown returned as he scoured the reports before him. His anxious eyes darted from papers to map and back. As we filed out, he glanced up: his sad eyes followed us with a look of helpless pity.

12

The German plan was as clear as daylight.

To forge an iron ring around Kiev, trapping the four Red armies inside it. Right now the pincer jaws were snapping shut. Kiev defenders were too weak and too few to hold the jaws open or break the rapidly-closing ring from without.

The city was doomed.

General Kirponos had lost radio contact with his High Command; so he had to rely on runners to squeeze through the gap and fetch orders. Since all his regular messengers had been either ambushed or sent to the front, he now had to depend on us raw Red Scouts. How could we kids know what fate awaited us!

The newly-arrived Scouts were excited by their mission. Now we could see some action, do our bit to win the war. Few of us slept soundly in our tent that night, for the darkness was full of bumps and bangs, flashes and flares, and the constant BOOM-BOOM-BOOM of distant guns. The front could not have been more than a few miles away, since the ground shuddered each time a shell exploded.

Bleary-eyed, the team paraded at dawn—having been woken up by the sergeant's WAKEY-WAKEY call. Far off, the horizon flickered with light—not from the rising summer sun, but from tracer bullets sending out strings of glittering pearls through the darkness.

The young sergeant with eye patch and bandaged head stood before our line of awkward recruits. His voice was surprisingly soft, as if shouting made his head ache.

'Right, *hloptsee*, go and get kitted out. Then fill your billycans from the mess and pair yourselves up for action. Be back in an hour, at o-seven-three-o.'

Still no one had explained our mission.

An hour later, the team trooped back to the tent, all dressed alike in baggy fawn trousers and jacket, felt boots, leather belt, and small boatlike cap. All we lacked for soldiering was a rifle.

'Ah, now you look like Red Army men,' said the one-eyed sergeant. 'By the size of you, you're all recent Young Pioneers, eh? So you can read a map and compass?'

At a few shouts of 'Yes, Sergeant!', he continued.

'I'm sending two pairs out today, at six hourly intervals. Your mission is to make contact with Captain Kravchenko's detachment at Lubny. These leather pouches here are for important papers—guard them with your lives. Right, any questions?'

'Is it dangerous?' asked a nervous voice.

'Very. Most runners don't make it.'

You could suddenly smell the cold sweat and fear on every face. No one said a word.

The young sergeant went up to the lad who'd asked the question.

'Look, son,' he said gently. 'This is war. To the death. Them or us.'

He paused after each sentence, moving along the line and looking each of us straight in the eye.

'If they break through to Kiev, it'll mean the cold-blooded murder of every man, woman, and child there— your mothers and little brothers and sisters. *We* are the last line of defence. And *you*, Comrade Pioneers, are our last link with the front.'

He paused to let the words sink in.

'Right, who goes first?'

Vera at once volunteered us: her, me, and Dinamo. She must have had her eye on a war hero medal.

The sergeant's one eye had a pained look—whether it was the dog, the girl, or the burns-scarred boy, he didn't say. He just muttered awkwardly, 'I hope that mutt doesn't yap.'

Then, drawing himself up, he added, 'Keep to the road and use your compass: you're heading five degrees north-west; target Lubny. Steer clear of German patrols. If you get caught, ditch the pouch and pretend to be locals. Say nothing. Should they cotton on, expect the worst.'

The worst? What was 'the worst'?

We didn't dare ask. Yet at heart we still didn't fear 'the worst'. People were people. Face to face, they'd surely not shoot teenagers. Would they?

Vera took charge of the leather pouch. She was boss, I was her batman. Dinamo her foot soldier. I didn't mind too much as compass- and map-reading weren't my strong points.

We had only five miles to cover. It sounded simple. The Red Army was holding out; we weren't crossing enemy lines; all we had to do was follow the Kiev–Brovar dirt track road.

All the same, I couldn't help asking Vera the big question that nagged at me: 'Why was he sending out pairs at six hourly intervals?'

Vera shook her head.

'If one doesn't make it, another might,' she said matter-of-factly.

Typical Vera. Blunt, fearless. Know-all.

No 'Don't worry, Vova. We'll be safe'.

It was such a beautiful summer's day, the promise of a real scorcher. One of those hazy, warm, tranquil mornings, with skylarks singing and swooping above the fields, that banish every care in the world.

We jogged along the dusty country road, Dinamo leading the way, wagging his tail as if out for a morning scamper. Far to the left we could see plumes of black smoke, like geysers spurting up from Hell's bubbling cauldron. Though we could only guess, they were probably tanks and batteries being blown apart, villages set alight, trucks exploding on a mine or shell.

After a mile or so, the track ended abruptly in a crater—a giant spoonful of earth gone missing. That was just the start.

Soon we ran into the debris of war: a huddle of empty huts beside the road, all shot to pieces; burned-out tanks, dead horses, bloody and bloated, mangled trucks, and piles of steel helmets all bearing red stars. A few old women were wandering among the shattered homes, trying to rescue their pitiful bits and pieces. One was gazing mournfully at a dead cow and three-legged calf that lay beside its mother, moaning and twitching in agony.

Aware of our important mission, we skirted the village and hurried on, stunned and horrified.

As we were picking our way along the pock-marked road, we suddenly heard a new sound amidst the boom-boom of guns. It was the all-too-familiar whirr of planes.

'Stukas,' said Vera knowingly. 'Quick, into the trees!'

A grove of silver-birch trees stood a hundred metres away—like a ring of dancing girls, so slender and graceful in their silver smocks, their green plaits whirling in the breeze. I remember Mum once saying that silver birches were the souls of dead maidens; if you break off a branch, hollow it out and make a flute, the dead girl will sing to you.

Such beauty amidst such horror.

We took shelter beneath the canopy of fluttering green leaves as the Stukas roared low overhead. Dinamo lifted his muzzle and barked loudly as if wishing to bite their tails. Vera and I watched in terror as the vultures dived upon the broken village we'd just passed, spitting fire and dropping bombs.

Why? For Christ's sake! Why kill old women?

Onward Christian soldiers . . .

As the planes veered right and disappeared over the steppe, we ventured out of our leafy shelter and walked on. Both of us were shaking as if the day had suddenly turned cold. Even Dinamo seemed to cower, his long tail trailing between his legs.

We passed more villages, almost all deserted and destroyed. Soon, however, we came upon something that, in a flash, revealed to us the whole horror and cruelty of war. The smell hit us before the sight.

From a distance it looked like a carpet of red-brown logs strewn across the track—hundreds of them, some piled on top of each other. By the stench, they must have been there for weeks: men and horses, horses and men—it was hard to tell which was which.

'Vova! Look away and follow me,' said Vera, trying to keep her voice steady.

She turned her own head away from the rotting corpses, pinched her nose and dived into the tall feather grass beside the track. I could tell from her heaving shoulders that she was crying. But she blundered on, angrily shoving the grass aside and clutching the precious pouch. Her knuckles were ivory white.

We made a wide detour, rejoining the Lubny road several hundred metres further on. We didn't glance back.

If the scenes behind us weren't bad enough, what awaited us ahead was to be stamped on our minds forever . . .

13

We reached Lubny at about two without further mishap —apart from the havoc caused by bombs and shells. To make base, we had to ford a broad river, the Sula, one of the Dnieper's many arms. Luckily, soldiers had bound logs together to make rafts and we were ferried across after producing our Scout papers.

In his dug-out, Captain Kravchenko handed over orders from High Command, and Vera stuffed them into her pouch.

'That son-of-a-bitch has brought you luck,' said the captain, ruffling Dinamo's wiry fur. 'Not many scouts get through.'

Then, with a wry smile, he said ominously, 'Even fewer make it back. Start the return run under cover of darkness and you'll stand a better chance. Till then, go and refresh yourselves. Oh, and by the way, if you do get back, tell the people of Kiev we'll *hold* the line . . . till our last drop of blood!'

He was only a young fellow, with a wispy beard and moustache beneath a potato peasant nose. He might have been nineteen, one of those country lads just starting college a few months back, looking forward to marrying his childhood sweetheart and settling down to a peaceful life as farmer, engineer, even violinist in some big orchestra. Who knows?

Now, if he looked the future honestly in the face, he saw either Death or Captivity. And captivity meant being stuck behind barbed wire on open land—no huts or beds or toilets. And no food either. Most POWs starved to death. As an officer, he must have known of Stalin's recent Order No. 270, condemning anyone who fell into enemy hands as a traitor.

Prisoners could expect no mercy from either side: shot in the back by your own or shot in the chest by the enemy.

While he was speaking, Captain Kravchenko's words were muffled by explosions and the whine of flying shells. The front line was obviously very close because we could feel the ground shake and clearly hear the rat-tat-tat of machine-gun fire and the pop-pop-pop of rifle bullets.

The barrage was so loud that, as we left the bunker, we scurried hands on heads towards the nearest tent—as if it would rain fire and lead at any moment. The mess tent was deserted apart from the cook. If we expected a bowl of hot *kasha* and hunk of black bread, we were out of luck.

'Sorry, *rebyata*,' said the cook without taking his hands from his trouser pockets. 'We haven't eaten in days. We're expecting supplies at any time. But, then, we've been expecting them for weeks . . . '

He flung a hand in the direction of the smoking battlefield as if no further words were necessary.

'If you want to make yourselves handy,' he continued, drawing on the fat shaggy roll-up and blowing smoke from one corner of his mouth, 'the sawbones could do with a hand—over there, down by the river.'

We thanked our lucky stars we had had breakfast that day; these men were starving, getting by on roll-ups and their daily ration of one hundred grams of vodka. You could see HUNGER writ large in their hollow eyes and cheeks.

The least we could do was muck in till dusk. Vera strode off quickly towards the river with me in tow. We were surprised to see no medical tents, no sign of medicine or drugs, just a single trestle table full of knives, tin cans, lint, and coloured bottles. What we did see made us wince and swallow hard.

Wounded men were lying on the ground, hundreds upon hundreds of them, evidently waiting to be ferried across the river to waiting trucks. There were so many, it would take ages to carry them all across on the tiny makeshift rafts. And scores more were being brought in all the time. Clearly, some had been there for days.

A woman orderly walked among the wounded, doling out words of comfort; she seemingly had nothing more to give. Many had been badly burnt.

Yet not one of them was moaning as they sat or lay there on the grass. Why didn't they complain? Why didn't they groan or cry?

But that wasn't the most tragic thing we saw.

Food supplies suddenly arrived: sunflower oil, vodka, potatoes, and loaves of bread. As the food was being unloaded from the supply barge, just thirty metres from the badly-wounded men, they rose up—yes, even the dying rose up as best they could—and, in an inexpressible stream of suffering, hurried towards the food.

A man without a jaw swayed as he hauled himself up; a soldier with a smashed arm raised himself on his good arm; those with burnt faces stumbled after the others, following the hubbub. They held out their hands like begging bowls. And as each wounded man stood up, he left behind a pool of blood upon the grass.

Not one cried, not one moaned. They were all dumb, as dumb as the poorest of the earth's creatures. And all had deep-set, expressionless eyes, eyes that had seen the horrors of war. They had fought with the white hot flame of patriotism.

That was something the Germans would never understand.

And, ultimately, no matter what it cost, *they would win*. For they were defending *their* homeland, *their* farms, *their* mothers, *their* children.

If there was one moment that changed our feelings about the war, this was it. The sight and conduct of those badly-wounded soldiers. They swept away all doubts about Germans possessing human feelings—of pity, love, shame. They filled us with a hatred and a determination to give everything we had to win the war.

> 'Kill a German, kill a German,
> Every time you see one!'

14

Never before had I been so relieved to see the dying of the day, a sunset of long angry red lines mixed with dense black gashes. At last we could escape this hell-hole back to Brovar. The only fly in the ointment was the late arrival of the second pair of Scouts.

'They should have been here by eight,' I mumbled to Vera. 'Maybe they've holed up somewhere till dark.'

'It doesn't matter,' she replied. '*We've* got the Orders and *we'll* hand them over safely. We'll probably run into them on the way back, spare them this place.'

She was right, as always. And we looked forward with a tingle of excitement mixed with fear to the journey home.

If it hadn't been for the cacophony of battle thunder and the streaks of man-made lightning, it could have been one of those summer nights made for fishing. A full moon smiled down on friend and foe alike, the river caught the moonglow and spread it sparingly over the rippling waves, so that the dark waters glistened and gleamed with a thousand tiny stars. Larch and pine upon the distant bank loomed up like phantom warriors about to plunge into the deep.

And here we were, mission half accomplished, about to set off for home. We had to carry Dinamo on to the raft; he hadn't found his sea legs on the first trip, and had yelped in fear. We couldn't risk him giving the game away.

'It won't be long now,' our ferryman grunted as he poled the raft across the tranquil river.

He let the current take us downstream, then braked hard with the pole, pulling, heaving, shoving off whenever he touched the river bed.

We thought he had been referring to our safe landing on the other side. But he continued, 'I reckons we're cut off good and proper. Them Fritzes are all about us. You young'uns'll be lucky to get through.'

'How do you know?' asked Vera crossly, and not a little anxiously.

'I seen shadows moving in the trees, heard foreign talk on the breeze.'

'Then why don't they attack?' I asked.

'Ah, he's bidin' 'is time, he is,' he muttered. 'Snap them jaws shut and swallow us down like the monster *Chudo Yudo*.'

Soldiers' tales, I thought. The dark always plays tricks with your eyes. He probably believes in wood demons and mermaids as well as *Chudo Yudo* monsters. We'll be safe with Dinamo to protect us.

Once beached, the raft held steady for us to hop off; we thanked the old fellow as he poled his way back. He said nothing until he was out of the shallows. Then suddenly he let out a sharp cry, crumpled up and slid over the side with hardly a splash.

We were so scared we ran for dear life along the river bank, dodging from tree to tree. We didn't stop until we were well away from the crossing point. Then, out of breath, we squeezed into the hollow of an uprooted willow tree.

'Where's Dinamo?' Vera said, looking all about.

'I thought he was right behind us.'

We both peered about anxiously, each silently blaming the other for letting Dinamo down. How could we have deserted our companion, caring only about our own safety? We'd left him to the mercy of the Germans—and they never showed anyone, man or dog, an ounce of mercy. We looked at each other accusingly. Finally, Vera spoke.

'Well, we can't go back for him. He'll have to find his own way home.'

Home? Where was home? War made us homeless in our homeland.

As we peered out of our sandy dugout, we could see in the river bend a dozen or more black figures with long rigid shadows beneath their arms; they were spread out like sentries all along the bank—obviously searching for us!

What were we to do? To reach HQ we'd have to break through German lines. Yet somehow we had to deliver the pouch. Kiev's fate might depend on it.

'Right, Vova, Be Prepared!'

'Always Prepared,' I replied automatically to the Pioneer salute.

'This is what we'll do,' she said. 'Follow the river downstream till we're clear of Jerry, then double back overland to reach HQ. Let's go.'

Oh yes, dead easy. As if signposts would guide us along the way: 'This Way to Company Headquarters . . .' But I had no better idea.

We listened hard for a few moments. A nearby owl hooted, the river lapped and gurgled, an ancient oak's branches creaked, a thousand eyes seemed to gleam from behind every tree. Odd, isn't it, how the weirdest thoughts enter your brain at the most unlikely moments. For some reason, I recalled a Pushkin poem I'd learned at school. How did it go?

> An oak tree green at river's bend,
> Its band of gold doth there suspend,
> Chained to a cat as wise as can be,
> Who day and night walks round that tree.
> To the right he treads—a song to sing,
> To the left he springs—a tale to spin.

Not that I expected to see Baba Yagá in the doorway of her hut on hen's feet. Still, at least she was *our* witch and might give us a magic ball of string to lead us through the forest.

We scrambled out of the hollow, caked in mud and sand, and loped off like two hungry foxes from clump to clump, tree to tree, shadow to shadow. There was no sign of any dog—nor 'cat as wise as can be'. Just us, sister and brother, boss cat and faithful friend.

We were lucky to have Comrade Moon to stop us falling down ditches and into creeks. After hugging the riverbank for a mile or so, we turned inland, making our way through a sweet-smelling pinewood. Vera kept consulting the compass whenever a shaft of moonlight filtered through the lofty trees.

'If we carry on due west,' she whispered, 'we should be running parallel to the Brovar–Lubny road, out of reach of tank and truck and motorbike. We'll swing round and rejoin the highway at the first village we came to yesterday—the "three-legged calf" one. Best foot forward.'

That Vera. She'd make a good general.

There was no sign of life in our neck of the woods— apart from a family of wild boar who ran off grunting and wheezing as if *we* were The Enemy.

It was tough going and we were both soaked in marshy water, smeared with mud, cut by stones, stung by nettles, and torn by brambles. We limped along as best we could, our teeth chattering in our heads despite the beads of sweat on our brows. It must have been nearly midnight, for the moon was directly overhead. We had veered right and could see a gap in the tree shadows not far ahead.

'The village should be just through the trees,' Vera hissed, pointing ahead. 'As quiet as a mouse from now on.'

I followed her, bent double, as we emerged from leafy cover. She was right. Ahead was the cluster of tumbledown log huts—more down than tumble, looking miserable in the broad splash of moonlight.

Talk about taking a sledgehammer to crack a nut! All that remained from German bombs were piles of splintered beams mashed into matchsticks. No sign of life—or even death. The dead cow and tormented calf had vanished into thin air.

As we crept closer, however, we could make out two wooden poles on a mound at the end of the village. From their uprights dangled long dark sacks that swayed in the gentle breeze. They certainly hadn't been there before.

Nothing else stirred.

Curious, we edged forward, holding our breath, until we were able to see them clearly.

With a gasp of horror, we both recognized the sacks at the same time. They weren't sacks at all! They were the second pair of scouts, Oles and Alyosha. They were hanging from a scaffold!

15

I'd never seen a hanging corpse before. It must be a horrible way to die, done more for show than easy killing. The bulging eyes, broken necks, and swaying bodies were meant to be a lesson to others.

'That's what happens if you don't play ball with us!'

Poor skinny Oles and lanky Alyosha wouldn't be playing ball with anyone again. I wondered if the Germans had tried to torture any secrets out of them. I stepped closer.

'Don't touch them!' cried Vera. 'They could be booby-trapped. Come on, let's get out of here.'

As she pulled me away, she muttered, 'At least the Fascists didn't get their hands on the Orders.'

We hurried out of the village, keeping to the shadowy side of the dirt track, beside the ditch—just in case we had to dive for cover. All was as still as death. The moon remained our trusty guide, lighting up the road ahead and fields on either side.

We had not gone far when Vera stopped, one hand on my arm, the other pointing ahead.

'What's that?' she whispered.

About a hundred metres down the road we could just make out a dark figure moving slowly along, wandering from side to side, as if trying to pick up a trail. It was too small for a man, more like a fox or wolf. The animal kept halting to sniff an old pile of horse dung or a tree stump beside the road, then darting forward, as if assured it was on the right track.

It didn't notice us behind it.

We had almost caught up with the sinister figure when, suddenly, I recognized it. I had to stifle a laugh of relief.

'Why, it's that old scallywag Dinamo,' I whispered.

No detours for him. Just dead straight, as the crow flies! Right through enemy lines.

When he looked round and spotted us, he came bounding over, wagging his long tail and licking our hands and faces. Then, as if to say, 'Follow me!', he plodded on ahead, glancing back over his shoulder every few paces to make sure we were behind him.

We ran into no more German patrols. But if it hadn't been for our dog scout, we could easily have been shot by our own trigger-happy sentries. Fortunately, they lowered their rifles when Dinamo barked at them, and let us through.

Despite the hour—it was three in the morning—General Kirponos was still awake, hunched over his maps and smoking his foul-smelling *mahorka*. He was obviously glad to see us, though upset about our two dead comrades.

'So young,' he sighed. 'This war will kill more children than all wars lumped together. That's the greatest tragedy.'

He pulled out a single thin paper from Vera's leather pouch. His fingers were shaking as he read it. We could see the surprise, disappointment, and anger in his eyes.

'The man's mad!' he muttered to himself. 'He'll be the death of four armies!'

Only later did we learn that the 'madman' was Stalin. He had refused to abandon Kiev even though it left his armies trapped in the Kiev pocket. They would have to fight their way out. It was futile—*and* stupid! Never would so many men be killed or captured in a battle for a city— over three quarters of a million. Old 'Bricknose' would die with his men; some say shot by his own pistol.

For the moment, however, General Kirponos's concern was to save what he could. And we were his immediate priority.

'Right, youngsters. Well done. You must be dead beat. Go and snatch forty winks. By dawn I want you and the rest of your team out of here and back in Kiev. Understand? There's slightly more chance of survival there.'

We were deflated. Our heroism at the front was all in vain. Our services were no longer needed. Still, if General Kirponos wanted us back in Kiev we would obey—without question.

Next morning early, a truck was waiting to drive us the short distance from Brovar to Kiev. We arrived back at the Dinamo Stadium safely, much to Coach's surprise. He appeared to be the sole guardian of the football pitch.

'Did you win your away match?' were his first words.

'We did, Ivan Ivanovich,' replied Vera. 'But victory came at a high cost: we lost two comrades, Oles and Alyosha.'

Coach sat down hard on a bench beside the running track, and held his head in his hands as Vera told him the story of our trip to Lubny and back. Strange, we could never imagine him crying; when she described us finding the two bodies, he did his best to hide it.

He pressed his hands hard against his cheeks, mouth, and eyes. But tears seeped through his fingers and ran down over the backs of his hands.

We were all his children, after all. And he felt responsible for our lives—and deaths.

After a while, he cleared his throat, spat on the ground, and stared awkwardly at us, his tear-stained face naked to our guilty gaze.

'Never seen a grown man cry before?' he flung at us. 'Never be ashamed of tears. As Karl Marx said of prayers, they're the heart of a heartless world, the soul of a soulless life, the sigh of the oppressed. There's no shame in tears.'

He wiped his eyes with the back of his hand and coughed huskily.

'Right, that's enough. We can grieve properly after this lot's over and done with. There's no time now. From what you say we can expect the Germans at any moment. Today's the fifteenth of September. They'll want to take Kiev and get on the road to Moscow before winter sets in.'

We were both scared, even excited by the thought of Germans strutting down the main street. It was so hard to picture. Back in the canteen our goalie Abram asked a question at the back of all our minds.

'Ivan Ivanovich, why do Germans want our land?'

For a moment, Coach looked lost for words, as if replying to 'Why do birds fly?' Then, with a sigh, he said quietly, 'Let me tell you one of Tolstoy's little stories, son. He called it "How Much Land Does a Man Need?"

'Once upon a time, there was a wealthy peasant called Ploughman. One day he heard of the rich black earth in the realm of the Bashkirs beyond the Volga River. "They're a simple folk and you can take all the land you want," he was told.

'Sure enough, when Ploughman reached the Bashkir lands the people said he could have as much land as he wanted for a thousand roubles—"all you can walk round in a single day."

'Ploughman was overjoyed. "That's easy," he exclaimed.

'Yet, on the way he kept spotting more and more land: good soil for flax, a big pond for watering his fields, an orchard of apple and plum . . . He wanted it all.

'Before he knew it, the sun was going down and he had to run fast to reach the starting post before the day was out. He just made it.

68

'But as he sank down on his knees, his heart gave out. "I've grasped too much!" he cried.

'So they buried him: two metres from top to toe.

'That's all the land he needed!

'The only difference now,' concluded Coach, 'is that instead of a single grave, the Germans are digging millions.'

16

Over the next few days, bombs fell thick and fast. Like moles, we surfaced briefly when no one was about. For food we finished off scraps left in the canteen pantry: stale bread, sweet wafers, and tea. Goodness knows why, but there were stacks of Iris-Kiss-Kiss toffees. These we sucked to stop our body mice gnawing at our innards.

Then, all at once, the bombing stopped. A stifling quiet descended like a thick blanket. It felt so eerie. Suddenly, through the still air came a crackling and a drumming of fingers on a microphone. The street loudspeakers coughed into life. What would they say?

'*Kievlanye!* Citizens of Kiev!'

The voice was Russian.

Our spirits rose. The Red Army had won? Won the battle for Kiev? Was driving the Germans back? All was well? The war was over?

The next words were like the icy hand of death gripping our hearts.

'Citizens! The Red Army is defeated. We have saved you from the Reds. The great German nation under our leader Adolf Hitler is master of all Europe. Many true patriots are fighting side by side with our German brothers to liberate the Ukraine. Join us.'

Further crackling. Silence. Then another voice, that of a woman:

'Tomorrow at midday, the twentieth of September, the German Sixth Army under its valiant commander General Guderian will make a triumphal entry into Kiev. Every citizen is duty bound to greet them. That is all. Heil Hitler!'

'Is it true?' a voice asked.

Coach shrugged. He had already prepared us for the worst.

'What's true is true,' he said hoarsely. 'The Red Army may have lost a battle, but *not* the war. What's true is that the Germans will free us all right—of our grain, our cattle, our coal, our iron, our young women. They'll all be sent to Germany to feed their war machine.'

We glanced uneasily at each other. How did Coach know so much?

'If that's true, Ivan Ivanovich,' spoke up Vera, 'how is it that some Ukrainians are fighting on their side?'

I think she knew the answer. But she wanted the doubters to understand.

Coach shifted uneasily on his wooden stool.

'Yeah, well,' he growled. 'Some of our people are taken in by Nazi propaganda, they're infected by hatred of Jews and communists. But they are fools to believe Nazi promises of liberating the Ukraine. All the Fascists want is to take our land for themselves.'

I could feel in my bones that not everyone present was won over.

I wondered what Mum would have said. Would she have welcomed the German soldiers as fellow Christians, come to rid us of the Reds who'd killed her parents? Who'd caused millions to starve to death. Who'd tried to destroy our culture and our language.

I could hear her voice in my ear: 'Hitler can't be any worse than Stalin!'

But neither Mum, nor Dad, were here to whistle or cheer.

'What are we to do?' someone asked Coach.

It was a question on all our minds. No doubt on the minds of all Kievans at that moment. We couldn't get out of the city. We were stuck here under Nazi occupation. Should we play along or should we resist?

'What are we to do, comrades?' echoed Coach in loud, rasping tones. 'Why, our duty's clear. We are a team. We are Dinamo Kiev. We defend our Dinamo team and our city of Kiev. We'll carry on the war behind enemy lines, make life difficult for those murderers.'

He stood up, spreading his arms as if to rally any doubters.

'Our duty, comrades, is to serve our country.'

A nervous voice piped up, 'But if we don't turn up tomorrow, they'll shoot us.'

It was dead Alyosha's younger brother. He was trembling in the corner, close to tears.

'They've got to find us first!' burst out Coach.

He then seemed to have second thoughts. He knew *his* duty. But he was also responsible for *us*. Why take unnecessary risks?

'Well, maybe our best plan is to play along, size the beggars up. Know your enemy, same as in football. OK, lads. We'll go down to *Kreshchatik* in the morning and watch the parade of rats. Keep together: safety in numbers. We're a team, never forget that.'

No one disagreed.

So, at half past ten next morning we emerged, blinking, into the sunlight, like rabbits from a warren. In twos and threes we trooped after Coach as he strode boldly down the hill, through Frunze Square and along the boulevard that fed into the main thoroughfare.

It was a Kiev we'd never seen before. Already thousands lined the streets, herded on to the pavement by militia women wearing blue and yellow armbands. Some were gloomy, afraid, confused, standing nervously about as if forced to witness an execution.

Yet some were in party mood: they were waving little red and black flags; some had armfuls of flowers to press on the soldiers or toss on to tanks; some wore folk

72

costume as on May Day or a national festival. Here and there, old Ukrainian flags hung from open windows.

I was baffled. They couldn't all be Germans pretending to be 'our' people, shipped in overnight. How had all these Nazi sympathizers been living secretly in our midst? And so many of them!

We had brushed past scores of flag donors who'd tried to press their paper swastika flags on us. But many had gladly grabbed the Nazi flag: 'Like lemmings rushing to their doom,' muttered Coach.

Policemen appeared from nowhere in strange green uniforms. They were 'ours'—they spoke Ukrainian; yet they were working for *them*, they were 'theirs', in *their* uniforms, carrying out *their* orders.

It was all most confusing.

Our team of thirteen—Coach, three girls, and nine boys—huddled together on a corner of Lenin Square, just in front of the red granite post office. We had a clear view up and down the street and across the square.

People around us said little. There was no excited buzz typical of national holidays. Some eyed their neighbours suspiciously—in case the man or woman next to them was an agent *for* or *against* the Germans. Who could tell?

We heard them coming before we saw them. The pipes and drums of a band, then rasping trumpets and trombones. Music to chill or gladden the heart—depending whose side you were on.

The band passed. There was nothing in the music or uniforms to tell whether they were ours or theirs. But their faces gave them away: the smooth, sallow cheeks, round eyes, close-cropped hair. Definitely German.

After the band came another kind of music: the even rhythm of marching feet, hundreds of jackboots strutting along the road; then the rumbling bass drums and clashing cymbals of tanks crunching their way over the tarmac. A shiny black open car followed the soldiers and tanks; beside the driver stood a grimly smiling German officer, his right arm held rigid in the Nazi salute.

The marching men, the tanks, and the officer were all so foreign. Our own soldiers looked like farm boys who'd just pulled on their wrinkled boots and uniforms. Their faces were open, kind and simple, with high cheekbones and slanting eyes. The Germans were smart, efficient, arrogant, and sinister.

Reassured by the long column of soldiers, some of the onlookers felt bold enough to show their true colours. There were cries of *'Dobro Pozhalovat!' 'Wilkommen!'* They threw their flowers, even offered a drink from bottles of vodka! The soldiers refused, probably thinking it might be poisoned . . .

A few grey-haired women held up family Bibles, icons, or crucifixes, and pointed to the black crosses on the tanks. One woman even ran forward to kiss the black cross on a passing tank, as if it were a holy icon on a church wall. She was roughly shoved back for her pains. Yet she still cried, 'Brothers! Brothers! Crusaders! God be with you!'

On the other side of the square, a group of young girls in national costume was standing, waiting for the General's car. The ceremony had clearly been rehearsed beforehand. For, as the car drew up, music played and the girls did a folk dance, while a tall graceful young woman with long fair plaits approached the General bearing a gift.

It was a large round loaf of black bread upon an embroidered cloth; on top of the bread was a small bowl of salt.

Bread and Salt! The traditional welcome to guests. Hail the conquering heroes! Our saviours!

Whoever believed that was soon in for a rude shock.

17

Day Three of the New Order.

Despite the Occupation, no German had yet discovered our hideaway. Perhaps they didn't fancy a game of footy. Or else they didn't want to storm a bastion guarded by our band of desperadoes? Anyway, at any moment we awaited intruders.

But we did have one unexpected visitor. That he was one of us was evident because he was pally with Coach; and Coach showed him round our make-do home. The pair finished up in the old manager's office which Coach had turned into what he called his 'Operations Centre'.

To our surprise, and not a little envy from the Team, Coach came into the canteen and bellowed, 'Grechko, brother and sister, Ops Centre, smartish!'

As we got up to go, Dinamo followed.

'No dogs!' bawled Coach.

Poor Dinamo sat down on his haunches, whining as we went through the door.

'Not another scouting job!' groaned Vera as we trudged down the long corridor.

Sitting at the manager's desk was the newcomer. An unsmiling, unshaven man with tired bloodshot eyes that darted here and there, magpie-like; not nervously, more like taking in every detail at a glance. He was dressed in a long black leather coat, too bulky for his small, slim frame. Somewhat oddly, he was wearing a faded black cap, the sort that used to be fashionable with old revolutionaries.

Four letters came into my head: NKVD—the secret police.

Right on the button.

'This is Comrade Danko,' introduced Coach.

It had to be a false name. We all knew Danko from Maxim Gorky's story about the hero who tore out his heart to guide his people through the dark forest by its glow. We could imagine this man tearing out his heart for the cause—or anyone else's heart for that matter.

'He's a partisan,' stated Coach in a whisper, as if that was something important, but very hush-hush.

The secret policeman must have noticed our puzzled looks. He explained drily, 'A new phase of the war has begun. Generalissimo Stalin has ordered us to organize resistance behind the lines. And the Resistance is in our hands—the *Partisans*.'

He cleared his throat, leant forward as if letting us into a secret, and said quietly, 'We have two units, each more than a thousand strong, both under NKVD command. Operations in and around Kiev. Harry the Germans, make their lives a misery—and any traitor in league with them. ''Blood for Blood! Death for Death!'' That's our motto. Understand?'

We understood. But why us?

'Comrade Danko has brought us food,' said Coach with a sly smile to his Party comrade.

We guessed that anyone offering 'Bread and Salt' to the Germans would lose their bread—and probably their lives too, once Danko's units got their knives into them.

'But he wants a favour in return. Done by two brave, daring youngsters.'

Vera spoke up. As usual, for both of us:

'Anything for the cause!'

Not to be outdone, I added, 'Blood for blood!' scarcely knowing what it meant.

'Right. Now this is the plan.'

Comrade Danko outlined no plan. All he said was that next morning we were to be picked up by a bread van.

Where and why he didn't say. Our job was to carry a bread tray into some building, leave it in the pantry and return home.

Easy. The only hint of danger lay in his last words.

'Don't hang about. Get out pronto!'

If I'd known then the terrible consequences of our action I would surely have refused. But I didn't. And I, like Vera, felt proud to be chosen.

'Not a word to a soul!' said Comrade Danko, putting a grubby finger to his thin lips. 'And remember this: *if* you get caught, you know NOTHING. The lives of your comrades depend on you.'

Since we did know nothing, there was no sense in the Germans torturing us . . . But would *they* know that?

Next day at nine thirty on the dot, Vera and I were waiting outside the stadium, alongside the statue of Felix Dzerzhinsky, first head of the Cheka, as the secret police was then called. It was one of those late September days when the summer sun shone brightly, yet a fresh breeze heralded the icy blasts to come. Summer always handed over to winter without giving autumn much of a chance to wither leaves and flowers.

A dusty old van with B-R-E-A-D freshly painted on back and sides drew up. The driver, an old fellow in clean brown overalls and floury cap, wound down the window and snapped, 'Get in the back!'

We clambered over the tailboard and pushed through the canvas flaps. Once inside, we found ourselves surrounded by trays of freshly-baked loaves. The smell of new rye bread reached right down to the pit of our empty stomachs. To us, who'd not tasted bread in many days, the temptation to tear off a crust was almost irresistible.

But we were on a mission. We were partisans. Our duty came first. In any case, the old baker barked back to us, 'Don't touch the bread! *For God's sake!*'

77

Why 'For God's sake!' Was this manna from Heaven or what?

The old man drove slowly through the main streets, avoiding bumps and sharp bends wherever he could. Through a slit in the flaps we caught glimpses of small parties of rifle-toting soldiers on street corners, columns of marching men, and knots of our people, pasting notices, digging, shifting, clearing debris. Evidently, having knocked the city down, the Germans were now building it up—for themselves.

A few times we had to halt at road blocks. With much banging and shouting, German guards ripped open the back flaps: ''Raus! 'Raus! Scheisse!'

They seemed furious that we didn't understand. From their actions and pointing guns, we soon learned basic German. ''Raus' meant, 'Out'; 'Scheisse' obviously meant 'us'.

The soldiers yanked us out and threw us to the ground, while they jumped up and inspected the trays of bread. Each time the reaction was the same: 'Brot!' They scanned the driver's papers, frisked each of us roughly, and finally waved us on. The only words I recognized were 'Herr Schmidt' (whoever he was) and 'Continental' (our grand hotel on the main square?).

The last guess was about right, because when the van reached its first delivery point, we could see the edifice of the Hotel Continental. Through a narrow passageway at the side, the van backed into a small courtyard surrounded by leafy trees.

Beyond the yard on every side lay hideous black scarecrows that were once trees, shops, and houses. Yet the hotel was untouched. Not a scratch. We weren't to know that Hitler had chosen the hotel as headquarters for his Sixth Army Command, and the HQ for Erich Koch, Reichskommissar for the Ukraine. It was here that 'mad dog' Koch was to hatch his evil plans for the people of Kiev. His were the first posters declaring that for each German death, a hundred Kievans would die.

Two German sentries with Sten guns tucked under their arms banged on the tailboard of the van, shouting the familiar, ''*Raus, Russen, 'Raus!*'

No use telling them we weren't '*Russen*'—Russians.

We hopped down as the driver was presenting his papers. Like the other guards they grunted '*Alles in Ordnung*'; but they ordered the driver to stay put—just in case he had any thought of sabotage. Kids presumably were harmless. All the same, they searched us thoroughly for hidden weapons. Maybe they thought we had a Katyusha rocket up our jumpers!

As we went to unload the loaves, our driver hissed, 'Second tray down on the right!'

We asked no questions.

What with guns trained on us and men in unfamiliar black and green uniforms coming and going, we bowed our heads and kept mum. I was trembling so much I almost tipped the tray over. When I caught the look of panic in our driver's eyes, it suddenly dawned on me: there must be something hidden in the bread!

My God! What if we dropped the tray?

Judging by the reddening freckles on her pale face, the same thought must have been going through Vera's mind.

With one guard in front and one behind, Vera and I carried the heavy tray down a long dark passage and into a cool storeroom. What a relief it was to lower the tray—gently, gently—on to a food rack.

Remembering the order to get out quickly, we both hurried back down the passage and into the sunlight.

The two Sten-gun bullies obviously enjoyed jabbing us in the back with their gun barrels as we scrambled into the van. They were soon cursing as the driver revved the engine and blew dirty fumes into their faces before driving away.

Our return journey was much swifter and bumpier than the first trip. And we made it through the checkpoints without delay.

'Well done, kids!' said the driver at the stadium entrance. 'You'll remember this day for the rest of your lives.' He drove off down the hill.

A minute later we knew what he meant. For as we were passing through the gates we heard one almighty explosion. It made the very air about us tremble and the birds start up from the trees. The huge bang was followed by a tall chimney stack of smoke that slowly blotted out the centre of the city.

Coach came towards us with a big grin.

'My brave partisans! A blow for freedom. We'll make them pay!'

Oh no! They made *us* pay. A thousand, thousand times over.

18

Day Seven of the New Order.

On 26 September, notices appeared all over the city. They looked innocent enough. No cause for alarm. Certainly no clue as to revenge for the hotel blast.

They declared in German and Ukrainian:

> JEWS!
> All Jews are to report for resettlement
> at Kiev Dinamo Stadium. At midday on
> 29 September.
> Bring belongings and valuables.
> One suitcase only.

A poster was even stuck on the stadium gates.

We joked that our two Jewish players wouldn't have far to go or much to take. Their only belongings were two pairs of football boots! Abram Gorinstein and left-half Yakov Livshits didn't know what to make of the notice. Was it good news or bad? We all had mixed feelings.

Why pick on the Jews? Some of us even felt a bit resentful. What had they done to deserve resettlement? Why couldn't we all be resettled, away from this war? Somewhere nice and safe. Switzerland maybe.

In any case, both Abram and Yakov were more Ukrainian than Jewish; they weren't at all religious, always played on Saturday, the Jewish Sabbath; they ate pork sausages like the rest of us. The only tell-tale mark about them was their names. And Yakov was just about to change that.

'From now on I'm going to call myself . . . Ulyanov,' he announced.

We all laughed. Ulyanov was Lenin's real name.

'If Ulyanov can become Lenin, then Livshits can be Ulyanov,' said Yakov.

It was sound reasoning.

'I'm not going,' he continued. 'It's a trick to get rid of us, put us away in camps somewhere.'

No one shared his fears. Perhaps we just wanted to reassure him and Abram. In any case, Abram disagreed. As a goalie, he was always concerned with getting his angles right. He worked it all out like a mathematician.

'Look at it logically,' he said. 'What's the point of putting the Jews in camps where they've got to be housed and fed. Better make us work for our food on a farm or in a factory. Even send us abroad out of the way. If you ask me, we're far better off out of it in some neutral country, beyond the reach of war. It wouldn't surprise me if our rabbis have bribed the Germans, bought freedom for the Jews.'

'Well, I'm not going,' insisted Yakov Livshits-Ulyanov. 'I won't desert my mates. And I plan to play for Dinamo Kiev, not some foreign team.'

Few Jews, it turned out, shared Yakov's fears or wished to remain in Kiev under the Germans. The Jewish elders helped organize the exodus, assuring families it was only temporary, till the war's end. So people locked up their homes, boarded up the two synagogues, collected their valuables, and put on as much clothing as they could.

From our canteen window overlooking the ground, we watched throughout the morning of the fateful day as families trooped into the stadium and sat quietly on the terraces. We were amazed as the early morning trickle became a steady stream by ten o'clock and, by twelve, a massive torrent of bodies—little children, women, old men.

It was all so orderly, like a school playground when

the whistle blows. But where had so many Jews come from? It seemed as if the entire population of Kiev had turned out, claiming to be Jewish. By midday we had a bigger crowd than the first team usually enjoyed!

We all lined up to shake Abram's hand as he went off to join his mum and little brothers. Even Dinamo stood in line, wagging his tail and lifting a paw.

'Dogs know,' said Abram with a smile. 'We'll be fine. I'll write to you from my new home.'

But Yakov wouldn't change his mind. He hugged Abram and kissed him on both cheeks.

'See you after the war, Abrasha,' was all he said.

The full stands reminded us more of a festival than anything else. An excited babble of voices echoed round the stadium, nerves adding body to the noise. Children who wanted to play on the grass were gently shooed back on to the terraces—much to our relief.

They were an odd sight. Some of the wealthier families had sturdy brown cases which weighed them down. But most had wrapped up their belongings in cloth bundles which they carried over one shoulder. Even the little children bore their burden as they waddled along in their winter furs.

About half past twelve, long lines of soldiers jogged into the stadium and surrounded the running track, as if policing a football game. It all added to the unreal match-day atmosphere. But the mood swiftly changed when a column of black-uniformed men marched in through the main gates.

Though we didn't know it then, these were the notorious SS *Einsatzgruppen*—the Nazi executioners of 'Communists, Partisans, and Jews'. Slowly and surely they ringed the track, pointing their guns at the Jewish spectators.

For one horrific moment I thought they were going to

mow them down in cold blood. But then an officer barked a command to a group of elderly bearded men in broad-brimmed black hats; they seemed to understand German. And the elders set about organizing an orderly departure from the stadium, family by family. Mothers and children carried their luggage in one hand and held on tightly to fingers with the other.

It took about half an hour for the long straggly line to squeeze through the gates, herded by the soldiers. At their head were the elders in long grey coats and broad hats.

For some reason it reminded me of 'The Pied Piper of Hamelin'; the elders were the piper, their followers the little children.

'They're better off out of it,' muttered Vera, as if to calm fears.

She did not know the full import of her words. For we were *never* to see any of them again. It was only days later, when we were all gathered in the canteen, that Coach told us of their fate. *None of us believed him!* It was too terrible for words. Even now, I feel the shock of his words run through me like a knife in the stomach.

'Comrades,' Coach began hoarsely. 'Partisan Danko has asked me to give you some bad news. He wants you to know the true face of the enemy. In revenge for the Hotel Continental blast, the Germans rounded up everyone suspected of disloyalty . . . And shot them.'

Vera and I exchanged anxious glances. No one apart from Coach knew of our part in the blast. Luckily for us the Germans hadn't cottoned on to us either.

At worst we imagined a few dozen patriots had died. But Coach's next words stunned and horrified us all.

'About thirty-five thousand people, so Partisan Danko says.'

It was unbelievable.

Thirty-five thousand . . . How can you shoot that

number? That's half a stadium. What would they do with the bodies?

All sorts of hideous images passed before our eyes. People in mile-long queues waiting their turn to kneel down and be shot. A vast plain of corpses piled on top of each other. Babies cradled in their mothers' arms.

No, no, impossible: thirty-five thousand. Thirty-five thousand! We couldn't take it in.

Coach saw our looks of disbelief.

'Our comrades hiding in the woods witnessed the slaughter. It took two whole days, 29th and 30th September.'

The twenty-ninth was the day we'd seen the Jewish families at the stadium! Oh no, surely not!

'First the Jews,' said Coach, his voice breaking; 'next Communists, then a few thousand prisoners of war. The swine marched them to the outskirts of the city, to Babi Yar, if you know it. They lined them up by an anti-tank ditch one mile long, eight feet deep.

'First they stripped them naked and took their valuables. Then they ordered the victims to step forward on to planks at the edge of the pit . . . and they shot them in the back of the neck. Line after line after line after line. Head first into the ditch . . . '

His voice wavered. We half expected him to break down. But anger got the better of grief, and he let out a long string of curses that made our ears burn.

In the awful silence that followed, it was Yakov who eventually gave voice to the question in all our minds.

'How could so many go unresisting to their deaths?'

There was no reply. How could we, who hadn't faced death, give an answer?

But Death was everywhere. Death could strike at any time: today, tomorrow, the day after. Men had become beasts. And beasts took death in their stride. Like a mother deer sniffing her dead fawn on the forest floor, and moving on . . . That's how we were.

No questions. Just move on.

Vera's voice rang out in a husky command.

'Team—a minute's silence in their memory . . . Then we'll go and make the Fascists pay!'

19

Sooner than we thought a chance came 'to make the Germans pay'. To tell the truth, we had little say in the matter. Our food supplies had run out and, as unregistered hideaways, we didn't qualify for rations. In any case, the allowance was no more than a mouthful of bread a day. The Germans wouldn't waste food on those who didn't work for the Reich.

'He who does not work (for the Germans), neither shall he eat.'

Our situation came to a head one evening when a fleet of trucks and rocket-carriers rolled up at the stadium; they parked right in the middle of the pitch, churning it up— the heathens! A handful of sentries were left in charge of the vehicles. We could clearly see them strutting up and down, shining torches. But thankfully they didn't enter the building.

No doubt, next day we could expect Germans and their Ukrainian helpers—the *Hilfi*—to move in. They obviously saw the stadium as a good vantage point over the city. So if any district misbehaved—Boom-Boom!—it would get a rocket bashing.

We had to depart in a hurry. But where to? Coach made the decision for us. Down in the dark changing room that night he called a crisis meeting.

'This is it, team, decision-time. If we stay here, we'll be discovered and put through the mincer. There are plenty of spies around to betray me, Yakov, and God knows who else . . . '

He looked meaningfully at Vera and me before continuing.

'The rest of you will be forced to slave for the Master Race, maybe sent to Naziland. The city's crawling with Nazis and rats among our own people who'd betray us as soon as look at us. Even if we bump off one or two, they'd shoot a hundred kids in revenge. So what are we to do?'

He looked helplessly at each of us, as if expecting an earful of helpful suggestions. When no one said a word, he spelled it out.

'Our only course is to join the partisans. That way we can blow up bridges and railway lines, make life a misery for the Germans—just like our people did for Napoleon— and we won that war just as surely as we'll win this.'

We all agreed with grunts or shouts of 'Victory!' even if our thoughts spoke differently.

'A partisan guide's coming for us at midnight.'

Oh, so it was all planned! No discussion. We were now soldiers in the partisan army. Under orders to carry out any command without question. Blood for Blood! Death for Death! Even if it was *our* blood and *our* death.

Dinamo barked approval, drawing attention to himself in the corner.

'It's too risky to take the dog,' Coach said gently. 'He might bark and give the game away.'

We had no option but to agree. Dinamo obviously didn't.

When we shut him up in the canteen, he started howling loud enough to alert the sentries. His howls tore at our heartstrings. How strange that we should feel more pain at parting with a dog than with human beings. Perhaps it was because he was so helpless, so dependent on us.

'Bye, doggy. Don't blame us too much for deserting you, old son.'

Our only hope was that the Germans would treat dogs better than they did Slavs and Jews. But, then, how could you tell whether a dog was Slav or Jewish?

No one came for us at midnight. We waited anxiously in a clump of trees on the wooded slope behind the stadium. It was one of those wild nights in early October when the wind was high, driving swirling grey-blue clouds across the heavens. The clouds would bare the bright moon for a fleeting second, like a searchlight flitting across the land, back and forth.

Just the night for the witch Baba Yagá to be flying in her mortar, sweeping away her traces with a birch-twig broom.

We were numb with cold; all we had on were a thin jacket and trousers, even the girls. Vera had had to ditch her burnt rags and don baggy green fatigues. Our teeth were chattering loud enough to wake the whole German army.

It was getting on for three o'clock before a low whistle warned us of someone approaching. It was our guide.

He was younger even than most of us; and he was scruffier, dirtier, as if he lived and slept in the forest depths like a wood demon, ready to pounce on wayward travellers.

'Follow me,' he ordered in a shrill, still unbroken child's voice.

No greeting. No excuse for lateness.

He darted ahead, half-bent, bounding like a light-footed deer. We did our best to keep up, but Coach's gammy legs soon had him lagging far behind. In no time at all we were well strung out; Vera and the guide took the lead, the footballers formed the main body, puffing and panting as on the training pitch; and the three stragglers (Coach and two girls) brought up the rear. Vera and the wood demon made no allowance for the less nimble.

We kept to the trees for a mile or so, then halted for a breather in a ravine between sand dunes. It was several minutes before the back markers caught up. The air we gulped down had a strange taste to it. While the woods had the heady scent of early autumn, here the air was mouldy, sickly sweet, putrid even.

Full of the stench of rotting carcasses.

At the sniffy chorus, our guide said simply, 'This is Babi Yar.'

No more words were necessary.

I stared about in awe—as in a graveyard; and in horror—as on a corpse-strewn battlefield. So this is where Abram had breathed his last, where thousands of bodies lay rotting beneath our feet, where one of history's most terrible crimes had occurred.

'They covered them over in quicklime,' piped up the child's voice; 'to burn them up, eh?'

He spoke as if his eyes had seen it all. Nothing shocked him. Nothing was out of the ordinary. The sights of war had tempered him like steel. But *we* weren't tempered; *we* were still sponges soaking up each new horror. Though Vera and I had seen the ugly face of death, this unseen act was too gross to fit into our minds.

All that formed in my head was the stupid, even obscene thought: half a stadiumful of people lie beneath our feet!

'*Poshlee!*' said the young-old sweat. 'Keep up!'

Like the last of the Mohicans, he was untiring and sure-footed about the forest, never stumbling, never stopping to sniff the wind, never blundering into a village or highway.

After a while, the firm leafy forest floor gave way to a squelchy bog that sucked at weary feet and tripped us up on submerged roots. It wasn't long before we were all as muddy as our guide, and stinking like a muck heap.

At last, we caught the sweet smell of woodsmoke and the low buzz of voices. To our relief, we heard the 'sh-sh' and lilt of our own tongue. Suddenly, a concertina wheezed into life and a low mellow voice began to sing, beautifully, movingly. It was such a contrast to the awful memory of Babi Yar, the wind howling, and the fearful crack of twigs in the forest.

> 'The fire is flickering in the stove,
> Resin trickles like a tear from the log,
> And the concertina in our dugout
> Sings to me of your smiling eyes.'

Sentries in rough peasant clothes suddenly broke the spell; half a dozen rose from the bushes skirting a copse of silver birch. When they recognized our guide, they let us pass and we entered a clearing of small roughly-made haystacks, earthy tunnels and canvas tents. Round a fire was a ring of some forty men and women. Sitting side by side, with their backs to us, were the singer and the concertina player.

'Wait,' said our guide. 'I'll arrange some warm clothing.'

Off he loped into the blackness. Nobody paid us any attention as we stood, peering through the gloom. In the fire's glow we could see some people sleeping, some smoking, some listening to the figure singing the sad song.

I *knew* that voice.

So did Vera, for she put her hand in mine. It was cold and trembling.

As we listened intently, we both gave a start. At the words 'Four steps to death', my heart skipped a beat: the country roll of the 'r' was unmistakable. I couldn't help myself.

'Dad!'

As if cut by a knife, the voice stopped dead. Several faces glowing red with firelight turned towards us. I guess war witnessed many such tearful embraces—of loved ones thought dead, yet meeting in the most unexpected places, at the most unexpected times. Yet none could have been more moving than that between Dad, Vera, and me. It must have given hope to all about us, for I later saw moist eyes glistening in the glow.

And there was more good news. Mum was alive. At least, Dad had seen her recently.

'God knows where she is now,' he said nervously. 'Natalia Petrovna is a nurse in a partisan unit, helping to save wounded soldiers trapped in the German ring.'

It turned out that Mum and Dad had been buried in the boiler-room of the block of flats during the air-raid. Luckily for them, the bomb had also smashed a hole in the sewer roof beneath the street. Dad had led the survivors through the stinking sewer tunnel, crawling on hands and knees, until they had reached some iron steps leading up to a manhole cover.

'We didn't come up smelling of roses,' said Dad with a grim smile. 'But at least we were alive.'

Dad was overjoyed to see us. He dragged us into the ring of comrades round the fire, one on each side of him and put his arms about us. Then, signalling with his eyes to the concertina player, he sang as loudly as he dared:

>'Sing, concertina, never mind the storm,
>Reach out to joy that's lost its way.
>I'm warm in my freezing dugout
>Because of your burning love.'

20

If Dad was glad to find us alive, he wasn't at all pleased to see us among the partisans. We were soon to discover why.

First things first. The team was fed and clothed warmly in rough peasant left-overs: homespun shirts and trousers, felt boots, and shaggy lambskin coats. We didn't give a thought to wearing dead people's clothes or how they'd come down to us. All that mattered in the middle of a freezing night was to keep out the biting wind.

We slept soundly in our new kit, huddled together in straw ricks into which we burrowed like mice; we were too tired to let biting ticks and fleas bother us. Our new comrades allowed us to sleep in; they must have known footballers needed their beauty sleep.

At around mid-morning we were woken up and summoned to the camp fire where a big pot of *kasha*, potato soup, was bubbling away. If we wanted a wash, we were pointed in the direction of a slimy, stagnant pond covered in an icy crust. We decided that dirt and mud were good insulation against the elements.

The first winter snow was falling thickly, whitening the whole camp—all but the red and black blaze in the centre of the clearing. It gobbled up the snowflakes with a grateful hiss.

Dad was nowhere to be seen. And *no one* asked questions about someone's absence. A few figures, mostly women, were gathered about the fire, some dozing, some cleaning rifles, binding bast shoes, patching, darning clothing. A stout rosy-cheeked young woman was doling out spoonfuls of *kasha* into tin plates.

'Eat, eat, my little pigeons,' she cried cheerily as she thrust the steaming plates into our hands.

While we were eating the partisan commander returned and was ready to inspect the new recruits. Our guide of the previous night, Vanya, clearly held the boss in awe, if not fear. He referred to him as Sasha, though never to his face, he hastened to warn us.

We wondered what sort of man this Sasha was. We were in for a shock.

Vanya took us down into an earthy canvas-covered dugout. It was roomy enough to take all thirteen of the team and still leave a respectful distance between us and the commander. At first we couldn't see his face, for he was squatting on his haunches, head cradled in his arms—presumably snatching twenty winks. In any case the dugout was in semi-darkness, the only light filtering in through holes in the canvas top and from a foul-smelling shell case converted into an oil lamp, with a rag for a wick.

When the commander looked up bleary-eyed and growled '*Dobro!*', we realized . . . that *he* was *she*! Sasha was Alexandra, not Alexander.

She had dark curly hair, cut pudding-basin style like a man, dark rings round her black eyes that seemed to glow like live coals in the gloom, a dimpled stubborn chin and pale, sallow cheeks. Her tired face and fierce glare did nothing to disguise her pretty, youthful looks. She couldn't have been more than twenty.

I heard later that she was from a well-known musical family in Odessa, and was herself a promising concert pianist till the war cut short her studies.

Unlike the other partisans we'd seen, she wore a simple, light-brown army uniform, with a greatcoat draped over her shoulders. She reminded me of my interview with General Kirponos, except that *she* was far less friendly. Now and then she winced as she moved her hands, which were covered in bandages.

'*Nooo* . . . ' she groaned in despair. 'So we're down to snotty-nosed street urchins, are we? Pig-bladder kickers and their cheer-leaders! Well, I tell you now, *detki*, war's no game of football.'

She searched our faces for some reaction to her hostility. We tried to keep a respectful silence. When she was satisfied that we were not about to answer back, she gingerly lifted a vodka bottle with both bandaged hands, tipped out a tin mug full and downed it in one. Then she continued, 'If you join us, you kill or be killed, got it! And if you're cowards, I'll kill you myself. Now go and get armed. Report for duty at twenty-one hundred hours!'

Obviously not a soccer fan!

We hastily climbed up the steps cut into the mud wall and followed Vanya beyond the clearing to a bunker hidden by trees. This time a sentry stood guard over the hole in the ground.

He was an old Russian; a cigarette wrapped in newspaper dangled from the corner of his mouth, seeming to grow out of the tangled mass of yellow-white hair. If the commander was unfriendly, Timofei Timofeyevich was the opposite: cheery and as chatty as a chaffinch. He introduced himself as 'Cavalry Sergeant, Civil War, Comrade to the legendary Chapayev.'

'Welcome to the Arsenal, *golubchiki*. Welcome, welcome, my *fizkulturniki*! Who's for a pop-gun and who's for a T34 tank? No? Well, let's see: we've a 7.6 centimetre anti-tank gun, or a sharp bayonet for sticking into German guts. No more Stalin organs—oops, sorry—Katyushas.'

He laughed at his own joke, coughed and spluttered. Then, when he'd got his breath back, he said wistfully,

'Now, if only we had a team of horses instead of a football team, we'd give Jerry a run for his money . . .'

He twittered on as he led us down into his 'Arsenal'. We were astonished at the array of weapons lining the walls: boxes of hand grenades—his 'pomegranates', as he called them; scores and scores of rifles—'M1891/30s', empty vodka bottles full of some explosive mixture—his 'Molotov cocktails'; and a treasure chest of axes, chisels, and wicked-looking knives: jack knives, carving knives, bread knives, bayonet knives, long and short knives, double-bladed knives.

He explained that the partisans had rescued stocks from weapon dumps abandoned by the fleeing Red Army. They even had a few German guns—'Not as good as ours,' the old fellow said, spitting on the floor.

He was most put out, however, when he found that none of us had learned to shoot, slit throats, or rip open enemy bellies.

'*Chort vozmee!* What do they teach you in the Young Pioneers these days?'

For the rest of the day he gave us lessons in weapon handling: shooting (dummy) rifles, throwing (empty) grenades, slitting throats and sticking bellies (hay-filled sacks). God forbid we should ever have to try out our rough and ready practice on real, live Germans! But as Timofei Timofeyevich kept drumming into us, 'If *you* don't get in first, *he* will!'

When we broke for a fireside meal of boiled potatoes, Vanya told us more about 'Sasha'.

'Don't mind her gruff manner. She's brave and fearless, and an excellent leader. Someone who knew her at school in Odessa told us that she used to be terribly shy, wouldn't say boo to a goose. But she had a wonderful musical talent and such beautiful long fingers.'

Remembering her bandages, someone asked, 'What happened to her hands?'

'Well, the story goes that she married a fellow music student, a violinist, while at college, and they had a child—that must have been in '40; her husband went off to war in early '41, and she followed on with the baby and her mother. He got posted to the Brest Fortress and was one of the first to fall when the Fascists invaded.

'She didn't have time to get out. When the Germans marched into the village where she was sheltering, they tore the baby from her arms and tossed it down a well. Apparently, she still hears its cries in her sleep.

'After that, she changed, vowing to kill as many Germans as she could, and in the cruellest way. They reckon she's already done for a hundred or so . . .'

'What happened to her hands?' asked Vera.

'She got caught, in Novy Gorodok, not far from these Pripet Marshes. She and her partisan unit managed to blow up three Nazi officers. In revenge, the Germans shot three hundred villagers, mostly women and children—one hundred for each officer—and then burnt the village to the ground.

'But they kept Sasha for interrogation. First she was whipped until her skin was cut to ribbons; then, when they heard from a prisoner who "coughed" that she played the piano, they gave her a "piano lesson", otherwise known as a "Fascist manicure". Do you know what that is?'

We shook our heads.

'Well, they lay your hands on a table and push red-hot needles under your nails, one by one. Then they take a rifle butt to finish off the "manicure". You can hear your bones crunching and breaking over your screams of pain.'

We gasped at the very thought of such torture. Finally, I asked quietly, 'So she escaped?'

'No,' said Vanya. 'She was the only prisoner they let go. To show what music lovers they are . . . In any case, they had another reason for freeing her: they'd captured her mother. They'd use her and other women to walk in front of German soldiers when testing for mines. As long as Sasha saw her mother in the front line, so the Germans thought, her partisans wouldn't dare fire.'

What a story.

And yet so commonplace. Just one of many that turned ordinary, mild-mannered women and men into merciless killers, caring little whether they lived or died, eager to kill as many of the enemy as they could.

How could the Germans not see that the way they treated our people only made them fight harder?

21

Dad returned with some disturbing news for Vera and me.

His reconnaissance group had found a wounded soldier holed up in a ruined village. The story the soldier had to tell alarmed us. Out of earshot of the others, Dad told the tale.

'According to this fellow, a band of partisans passed through the village—but they weren't *ours*. They were *Ountsi*—Ukrainians who'd thrown in their lot with the Germans.

'But that's not all. This soldier was lying in a ditch bleeding to death; he thought he'd had it. Yet all at once, this *Ountsi* nurse hears his groans and comes to the rescue. There wasn't much she could do about his arm; it was hanging by a thread from his shoulder. She had no knife or scissors, so . . . God, she must be a tough 'un—she used her teeth to bite through the sinew and tear off the smashed arm. That way she stemmed the blood and saved his life.

'Now here's the interesting part. The soldier said the others called her "Natalia Petrovna"; and from his description it sounded quite like your mother, though rougher and tougher than the woman I married.'

I didn't know whether to laugh with joy or cry with shame. If it was true, the family was now split, on different sides, sworn enemies who'd have to kill each other if need be!

'At least Mum's alive,' I got out, breaking the awful silence that followed Dad's news.

'She's better dead!' muttered Vera, turning on me. 'Those *Ountsi* are worse than the Fascists, they kill their own people; they're traitors and bandits!'

How war had hardened Vera. Fancy wishing her own mother dead! I could tell she was modelling herself on the partisan commander, Comrade Sasha. Victory at any cost. No, no, I could never turn against my own mother, no matter what. I'm sure that, despite his Party duties, Dad felt the same.

But neither of us said a word. War was war: no room for sentiment. At least, not out loud.

That night, Vera and I were to go on our first patrol. The partisan band consisted of three of the team and half a dozen seasoned scouts. Sasha herself was to lead the group. Old Timofei grudgingly issued us each with a rifle and a round of bullets. 'Don't waste them!' he warned. 'Shoot to kill!' I hoped it wouldn't come to that. I had no idea how I could shoot another human being.

Sasha summoned us all to her bunker for a short briefing.

'We lost a young comrade yesterday, Zoya Novik. She was one of our best snipers; and we can't afford to lose good soldiers. When she twisted her ankle we had to leave her behind in a "safe" hamlet.

'Germans are prowling about the area, so our task is to get her out before they find her. It should be straightforward, there and back quickly. It'll give the kids a taste of night patrol. Let's go.'

It was already dusk as we set off, single file, through thick snow. We were supposed to step in each other's tracks so as to disguise our numbers.

The going was harder than before because we couldn't see or feel what was underfoot. If we trod on an icy crust or snowy clod, we could find ourselves struggling up to our knees in freezing quagmire. Luckily for us, Sasha knew the way, leaping from tuft to tussock, sticking to the high ground, skirting the bog. It was such a bright moonlit night we could see far ahead. We'd soon spot a German patrol against the pure white backdrop; but, then, they'd just as easily spot us.

To our relief, nothing moved. It was so still and peaceful. The only sound came from our breaths, puff-puff-puffing like a chugging goods train, from our feet crunching down the virgin snow, and from old Red Nose Frost whistling and crackling through the silvery branches.

Now and then, Sasha stopped, raised a gloved hand and harkened to the wind blowing in our faces. She was listening out for unnatural sounds: an owl that wasn't an owl, a crack that wasn't from ice-bound trees, a voice that wasn't ours.

Snow began to fall, silently, hurriedly; it seemed wrong to spoil the delicately embroidered snowflake pattern beneath our feet. We had been trekking for a good two hours and I was feeling footsore. Luckily, our journey was almost done, for in the distance, through the bridal veil of pearl-studded snowflakes, I could now make out the onion dome of a village church.

It stood on a hill above the little cluster of huts, like a fairy-tale paradise above the squalid peasant earth. Despite the snow, the golden cupola gleamed like the Polar star, guiding us to our goal.

We were more cautious now, bending double as we scurried through the snow. Yet, as we came closer, we could tell that something was wrong. We could smell trouble. Woodsmoke. But from old timbers; there was the sweet aroma, too, of straw and clay, not peat fires.

Thin wavy spirals of smoke were mingling with the snowflakes, one rising up, one falling down. Not the sort of smoke from stoves; in any case, there was too much smoke for house fires.

Sasha held up a hand again and waved us down. Alone she darted forward, zigzagging across the ground like a vixen hunting a hare. Though she kept low to the earth, dashing from tree to tree, anyone on the hill could have spotted the dark figure scurrying below. We held our breath.

But no shots rang out. No warning cries went up. No sentry sounded the alarm.

After fifteen minutes, she was back.

In a hushed voice, she said, 'The hamlet looks deserted: just ash and charred timbers. No sign of life. Let's see if we can rescue some food and clothing. Be on your guard in case of booby traps.'

We fanned out and started a search of each hut. There wasn't much to find. The Germans had ransacked the place before burning it down. No bodies lying around, apart from a dead dog in an icy pool of blood.

Sasha seemed less concerned for the fate of the villagers than for her comrade Zoya. She was convinced that Zoya had neither escaped, nor been taken prisoner.

'Germans don't feed unwanted mouths,' she growled.

We'd searched the smoking ruins of every hut. All that remained was the hillside church. The church was perched on top of a steep hill, above the huddle of huts, as if churchgoers had to go through pain and suffering, like Christ on his climb to Calvary.

Since the church wasn't likely to hold food or clothing, we hadn't bothered about it. Now we climbed the hill to the forbidding building.

Like the smouldering huts, it was ransacked and deserted. Not even an icon or cross left inside.

'Where are they all?' said Sasha.

She was obviously baffled at the lack of human life.

'You two,' she barked, 'nip round the back.'

Vera grabbed my arm and pulled me after her towards

102

the graveyard behind the church. It was even more scary because, at that moment, the moon sailed behind a cloud, leaving just a dim, fuzzy gloom. All we could see were dark burial mounds, uneven rows of graves, some with rusting metal crosses, some with stars and photos of the dead on the headstones.

All of a sudden, Vera halted, catching her breath. She pointed towards the tall rear doors of the church. Her strangled cry made my hair stand on end.

'What's that?'

I strained my eyes, but could only see a pile of rubbish heaped against the doors. It looked like bark-stripped logs.

At that moment, the moon popped out of its hiding place, mercilessly shining its spotlight on the doors.

I gave a yell of fear and hid my head in my hands.

The others came running.

Naked bodies, sheltered from snow by the roof eaves, were lying where they'd fallen, spreadeagled in their death throes. Shot . . . and bayoneted for good measure. Tiny bare arms still clung for comfort to blood-stained hands.

What shocked me most were the staring, horror-filled eyes; they looked like camera lenses recording the butchers at their vile work.

But that wasn't all.

Someone pointed towards the centre of the graveyard. We all followed the outflung arm. There on a mound stood a wooden cross. It must have been dragged from inside the church, for the wood was smooth and polished.

Upon the cross hung a slight figure. Its hands and feet were nailed to the wood. Jagged lines of dark blood ran down from the nailed flesh, and two almost straight lines ran from where the eyes had been, down to the chin, as if the figure had cried tears of blood before it died.

From Sasha's first sign of emotion, I guessed the figure must be Zoya. The snowflakes were swiftly taking pity on her. They quickened their pace and soon covered her with a modesty sheet, turning her long hair completely white.

'Poor angel,' said Sasha, her eyes full of tears.

Angel she was: of white stone, guardian to the dead. And inspiration to the living.

22

Revenge was swift and sickly sweet.

It was not hard to follow the tracks. The raiding party was on foot and their jackboots left a firm imprint in the snow. By the broad sweep of trampled snow they were about thirty in number, almost three times more than us. As if it mattered! Sasha was in no mood to scurry off home, tail between her legs. She was bent on revenge.

'We'll catch the swine. For Zoya's sake! And I'll make them pay!'

Sasha reckoned they had a couple of hours' march on us. The dead bodies were still warm despite the frost, and blood was thickly running still, spreading reddy-pink fingers into the melting snow crystals. Deep rust-coloured furrows across the plain suggested men hauling booty from the hamlet. Probably slaughtered pigs and goats, and sacks of grain.

Rings of black slush betrayed their resting places.

'Greed will be the death of them!' muttered Sasha.

After what I'd seen, even I was ready, no, eager, to kill my first German—and my second and my third, as many as I could get my hands on. Hammering at my brain was the angry thought: they aren't human, they're monsters, bloodthirsty vampires who had to be stopped before they tore the flesh from other young girls, ripped the hearts out of more little children.

Rage and pity lent us strength.

Within the hour we spotted black ants crawling across the skyline. They were moving slowly, lit up clearly by the full wintry moon.

'Proceed with caution!' came the soldierly command.

Not that it mattered. Snow muffled our footsteps, the wind was in our faces, not at our backs; and the Germans didn't seem to be on their guard. They had no inkling we were on their trail.

Soon we could catch the odd sound on the breeze: a shout, a harsh laugh, a curse, a sharp order. Another resting place—their last—enabled us to reach a clump of larch trees above our unsuspecting quarry.

We peered down from our perch, like crows upon their prey.

There were more than we'd anticipated—a good forty. All in olive-green uniforms, black jackboots, faded forage caps. Only the officer wore black: his smartness contrasted with the sloppy manner of his men. He sat apart, smoking and staring into space. He did not join in the jokey chit-chat.

The reason soon became clear. For words drifted up the slope to the larch grove: *'Smakuee . . . Kostya . . . Hloptsee . . . Gospodee . . .'*

Our language!

These weren't Germans, they were *ours*, Ukrainians!

The full horror of this slowly dawned on us. What sort of savages could kill and mutilate their own flesh and blood? Were they out to impress their German masters by their cruelty? Did they really think Jerry would pat them on the head and hand over the country to them?

'Hilfi!' hissed Sasha. 'I'll take the Nazi officer. Pick your own traitor and aim for chest or back. When I say fire, FIRE!'

The men were utterly unaware of the sword of death hanging over them. They were lounging back, smoking, guffawing, drinking from tin mugs—by the quick tilt of chins, the throat-burning drink was evidently *gorilka*, Ukrainian vodka.

We could see the German officer clearly, since he sat above the rest. He had removed his peaked cap and was wiping his brow and neck. The trek over snow was obviously hard work.

He had a large, brutal, close-cropped head with eyes deep set and full of contempt—whether for his men, the war, the country he was in, we couldn't tell.

All at once, he got to his feet and barked an order in German. That was the signal Sasha was waiting for. The soldiers presented a bigger target on their feet than on their backsides.

'FIRE!'

I pulled the rifle butt hard into my left shoulder and, under my breath, repeated old Timofei's instructions: hold steady, aim, squeeze, don't pull the trigger.

The butt bumped back into my shoulder. A wisp of smoke curled up from the barrel. That was it. Over and done with. Easy.

The man I'd aimed at looked up in surprise as if stung by a bee; he put a big hand to his chest and slowly slid to the ground in a ball, knees doubled up to his stomach.

Did *I* do that? He seemed so far away. Instead of pity, I felt a pins-and-needles thrill cramp my whole body. Instead of a falling soldier, I saw naked pink bodies piled high against the church door. Instead of congratulating myself, I quickly reloaded, put another bullet up the spout.

One up, one down! One shot, one hit! Not bad for a first timer.

The volley of rifle fire caused pandemonium among the men. Some sprawled unmoving in the snow, some were crawling on hands and knees; some were fumbling for weapons to defend themselves. No command came from the German officer: his face was a bloody mass of broken teeth, nose, chin, and hair.

Sasha had disobeyed her own order and gone for the face. Smack on the nose!

For the survivors there was nowhere to run. Nor did they see where our attack was coming from. Some tried to shelter behind grain sacks, but lead bullets ripped through sack, grain, jacket, flesh and bone. Grain mixed with guts spilled out as red-soaked bran.

After several volleys, the few survivors raised their hands above their heads. If they'd known we were only a tiny band of inexperienced partisans led by a concert pianist, they might have thought twice about surrendering. But the eight or nine uninjured, and the five wounded, were defenceless once they'd thrown down their guns.

Sasha ran down the slope, rifle at the ready. We followed, pointing our gun barrels at the frightened men. They clearly weren't expecting a dozen or so kids and women. When one of the wounded made a sudden snatch at a fallen rifle, Sasha put a bullet through his head.

'Anyone else feeling brave?' she cried.

No one was.

What happened next I'd like to rub out of my head, like chalk from a blackboard. In my innocence, I imagined we'd tend to the wounded, patch them up as best we could, and then march the prisoners back to camp for interrogation. But Sasha had her own idea of justice.

An eye for an eye.

'*Vee nashee* . . . You're *ours*,' Sasha said quietly. 'So tell us the size and location of your unit.'

No one said a word.

'Right, Tonya,' she said without looking round. '*Strelyai!*'

Five pistol shots rang out.

'Now we don't have to bother with so much baggage,' she said.

Her face smiled, but her eyes were hard and narrow.

'Come now, who'll tell Auntie Sasha what she wants to know?'

The silence was tense and deafening.

Sasha sighed.

'Verochka,' she said to my sister. 'Loosen tongues will you.'

When Vera approached her, Sasha whispered in her ear. As if in a trance, Vera marched to within six paces of the first prisoner and trained her gun on his heart. Perhaps it was disbelief at being shot by a girl who reminded him of his young daughter, but the man held out his hands, pleading, *Dochenka*, I've a girl just like you. Go home and play with your toys. War's a man's game!'

No one gave an order.

But a shot rang out and the man fell without a cry, a pained look upon his face. He was dead before he hit the ground.

That unblocked the dam. The remaining seven prisoners all started babbling at once; a few fell to their knees, crying, begging, 'Don't shoot, we're yours, we'll tell you . . . anything. Please don't shoot . . . '

Having brought them to their knees, Sasha suddenly lost interest. She turned abruptly on her heel, crying, 'Finish them off!'

Have you ever seen a grown man beg for his life? Tears in his eyes, hands outstretched or held together in prayer. Sobbing, imploring, begging you to spare him?

I could scarcely bear to look. I knew they were cold-blooded murderers. But didn't killing them make us almost as bad? In any case, Mum could be standing with them now; she was a traitor too.

'We'll show you Red mercy,' Sasha shouted, 'the same you showed the village women and children, and young Zoya. *Strelyaite!*'

Not every man died at once. One or two writhed on the red-white snow and had to be finished off with a pistol shot in the head.

'Let all Fascists know what awaits them!' was Sasha's parting comment.

23

Back in camp, I gave Dad a blow-by-blow account of the gruesome events. Dad was a softie, like me. Vera took after Mum.

Dad silently shook his head.

'What turns a shy pianist into a cold-hearted killer?' I asked.

He mulled it over for a few moments, sucking on it like a toffee; then he shrugged. It was beyond him, but he tried his best, as he always did when I asked questions.

'War, son, I guess. It turns the kindest heart to stone. When they see their loved ones die in torment, like poor Zoya, some just want revenge; they lash out blindly, give like for like.'

'That's easy to say,' I continued. 'I'm sure I couldn't cut out eyes and tongues, shoot someone in cold blood, gun down a defenceless person begging for his life.'

'You and millions of others, Vova. We were brought up to love our neighbour, to love workers of the world, to love all races. Others weren't. But now that some neighbours and workers have turned against us, we have to learn to hate. It's a hard, cruel lesson. But if we want to defend our land, our own folk, our family, we have to learn to kill.' He sighed deeply. 'We have to be as brutal as the enemy.'

'Like Comrade Sasha?' I said.

He didn't answer.

My thoughts at once switched to Vera, and I said no more. With every passing day I could see a change in her.

In the weeks and months to come I watched my sister turn into a model partisan. She never hesitated to carry out an order—whether shooting hostages or burning down a 'hostile' village. I often felt she went out of her way to impress Comrade Sasha with her ruthlessness: 'anything you can do, I can do better!'

Our mission was to hit and harry the enemy all the time, so that they never felt safe, anywhere. We'd dig holes in the ground, full of sharp stakes, and cover them over. We'd slit throats of sentries in the night—swiftly and silently. We'd pick off stragglers in a column of soldiers. We'd strangle men as they slept in their tents.

We made their lives such a misery that they jumped at their own shadow.

Of course, they hit back. When a partisan girl put a time bomb under the bed of Belorus Commissar Wilhelm Kube, and blew him to bits, a thousand innocent souls were hung on Minsk's main square. Kiev and Kharkov were sealed off, so that no food supplies could come in; people were reduced to eating dogs and cats. When these ran out, people ate crows and pigeons, made omelettes of rat droppings and human blood. Hundreds of thousands starved to death.

Many blamed *us*. For every German killed a hundred innocent Ukrainians died. That was Hitler's Order.

What should we do? Roll over and let them win the war? If we did our bit here, in the Pripet Marshes, it might sap their will and strength, bring closer the day when our armies would stand firm, then drive them back: at Moscow, at Leningrad, at Kursk, at Stalingrad.

In any case, we were under orders from Internal Security—even if those orders were cruel.

One day in late March, we were out on patrol; our instructions were to ambush a column of Nazi trucks taking supplies to a forward base. The night before we had mined the road. Once the front truck blew up, we'd toss grenades into the rest and make our escape in the confusion.

We feared they'd be up to their usual dirty tricks— using our women as a shield.

Whenever the Germans travelled in convoy, they spread a line of women prisoners across the road. The women were made to walk some twenty paces ahead of the soldiers guarding the convoy. Not only were the women likely to trigger our mines, they made it hard for us to fire at the enemy over their heads. Even Sasha had qualms about killing our women.

But what could we do? If the convoy got through, it could mean the death of hundreds, maybe thousands; it might turn the war. And our orders were to stop the Germans at all cost!

All we could do was set our mines deeper in the snow, so that only heavy wheels would set them off. It didn't always work. More than once I'd had to hide my face in my hands as, with a terrible scream, our—my!—mine had blown a woman's legs off or killed her outright.

On this particular morning, we were lying in wait on a wooded slope above the main Minsk–Kiev highway, just beyond a sharp bend in the road. An overnight snowstorm had covered our tracks and deadly handiwork. It wasn't long before we could hear the sinister buzz and drone of lorry engines, partly muffled by the snow.

They were moving slowly, like tractors across a ploughed field. As usual, I felt a tingle of excitement that made my index finger twitch nervously on the grenade safety pin. In my mind I went through all the actions to come: pull pin, count to five, throw; pull pin, 1,2,3,4,5, throw!

Vera was in a forward position alongside Comrade Sasha: it was their job to shoot down guards in front of the armed convoy. Very, very tricky because of the human shield. Sasha was grooming Vera as Zoya's replacement: she was a good shot and could be relied on. Most of all, she was merciless: she wouldn't hesitate to sacrifice our women if necessary.

As the engine whirr grew louder, a line of ten women, tied together, arm's length apart, appeared round the bend. They were shuffling along, obviously in great dread, heads down, searching the ground for tell-tale marks, knowing their next step could be their last.

I knew what they didn't know. They had another thirty paces to go to the first line of mines. I ought to know since I'd planted them myself. I held my breath. 'Please don't step on my mines!'

Those poor women risked being shot from front and rear, as well as being blown up on the spot! Even if they survived this time, they'd have to go through it all over again—again and again until one day: BANG! A mine would tear off their legs or blow them to smithereens.

We'd carried out the operation a few times before— with mixed success. Twice we'd halted the trucks in their tracks, and left dead Germans in the snow before beating a retreat. Once our mines had failed to go off, and we'd had to look on helplessly as the convoy passed.

On the last occasion, a week back, the mine-layers tried to repair their error by setting the booby traps just below the snow: the result was three bodies in the shield blasted across the road. The sight of torn women's bodies only fired us up; and we managed to destroy the entire column, blowing up the lorries with our hand-grenades.

That was why I was so anxious about the mines today.

To my relief, both the women and the soldiers trod over the mines safely. Now for the convoy . . . As the lead

truck's wheels hit the mine—BANG! CRASH! *Yolki-Palki!*
The driver went flying through the windscreen and the
truck slewed all over the track, blocking the road as it
caught fire and buried its nose into the bank.

That was the signal for us to hurl our grenades into
the other seven trucks, and for our snipers to pick off the
guards.

But something was amiss. For some reason our
commander seemed to have lost her nerve. Perhaps it was
the hostages. The guards had quickly sheltered behind
the frightened women, holding them fast as bullet-proof
screens. Most of the women were elderly and, to judge by
their clothes—long black felt padded jackets and brown
woollen headscarves—villagers.

They were wailing and crying out to us, 'Don't shoot.
For God's sake! Don't shoot!'

Sasha wavered. Her rifle drooped as she half stood up,
hesitating, her eyes wide with fear. We waited in vain for
her command. But nothing came. Just a strangled cry
which none of us understood. I'd never seen her like this
before. She was always so sure and fearless: a born
leader.

But Vera, realizing the danger, took control and shouted
out, '*Ogon!* Fire!'

She stood up, holding her rifle steady, took aim and
fired. Her bullets sprayed the tangled mass of women and
soldiers. The surviving soldiers thrust their hostages aside
and dived for safety behind the trucks.

Three women lay face down in the snow; two others
had sunk to their knees, unable to move, like rabbits
whose back legs are caught in a trap. Other women were
shaking their fists at us, screaming, 'Fascist swine!
Murderers!'

Vera ignored them. With no thought for her own safety,
she dashed forward to flush out the remaining soldiers.

115

She must have finished them off single-handed, for by the time we reached her the convoy was silent.

The trucks were all disabled, the drivers dead, the soldiers lying prone upon the ground or twitching in agony. Our orders were always the same: take no prisoners. So to the sound of whips cracking, Olga and Tonya finished off the wounded with pistol shots.

I couldn't bear to watch; it was a moment I never got used to.

When I finally looked about me, Sasha was nowhere to be seen. It was only when I heard sobbing and a voice crying, *'Mamulya! Mamulya!'* that I realized she was at the front of the column. While the others gathered up weapons, I ran quickly towards the cries, wondering what was the matter. But I stopped short a few paces from her.

She was sitting in the snow, rocking to and fro, moaning and crying. In her lap she was cradling the head of a dying woman. The woman was bleeding badly from the chest and scarcely breathing.

I'd never seen Sasha like this before: so tender, so weak, so womanly.

Gently she brushed back the thick iron-grey hair from the woman's face and, with her other hand, was trying to stem the flow of blood with a handkerchief. Suddenly, in a weak voice, the dying woman muttered a few words. Apart from Sasha, I was the only one who heard.

'Alexandra, why? How could you shoot . . . your own mother?'

The effort was obviously too much. The woman's head fell back and she lay still in Sasha's arms. Tears ran down the daughter's cheeks and fell softly upon the mother's pale brow.

Sasha hadn't said that the shot wasn't hers; that she'd recognized her mother; that she hadn't been able to shoot; that she'd given no order; that she'd done nothing.

Her tear-filled eyes looked up as Vera approached. They held no reproach, no blame. All Sasha said was, 'Good girl. You did right.'

24

My time with Dad and Vera in the partisan unit was unexpectedly cut short. One day in early July I was summoned to Comrade Sasha's bunker. I thought she was about to send me on another dangerous mission, but she wasn't there. Instead, I saw a vaguely familiar, unsmiling figure. It was Unit Commander Danko.

'Comrade Vladimir!' he said in greeting.

My exploits must have earned me the chummy title; but I guessed it was sugar to coat the pill.

'I hear you and your sister are crack marksmen. What's your tally?'

To put me in Vera's league was a step too far. If she was in Division One, I was somewhere near the foot of Division Ten. Anyway, I had no idea how many Germans I'd killed. What's more, I didn't care. Unlike my friend Yakov, I didn't cut a notch on my tally stick for each dead Jerry—he cheated anyway.

Danko wasn't *really* interested in my tally. For he got down to business straightaway.

'I've got good news for you. New orders. You're to return home with the team, back to Kiev.'

I tried not to show surprise, let alone delight.

OK. Whatever serves the cause. I obey orders.

'Yes, sir.'

After a brief thought I added, 'I suppose we can kill Germans more easily there than here.'

'You aren't going to kill any Germans. Not for a while anyway . . .'

His next words nearly knocked me over.

'You're going to play football.'

I stared. This was *war*time, not *play*time. The last big-time football match in Kiev was when Dinamo had played Tbilisi at the new Stalin Stadium. War broke out the very same day! Since the Georgian Tbilisi team won we held them responsible for the outbreak of war.

Seeing my look of disbelief, he explained.

'Tell your team-mates this. There's a German bigwig by the name of Schmidt who's taken over our main bakery. He lived in Kiev before the war and is keen on football; apparently he's got a soft spot for Dinamo and wants to form a team from what's left of its players. They'll play for him at the local stadium, Zenith, on Kerosene Street. D'you know it?'

I remembered Schmidt's bakery all right. We'd used their van when blowing up Hotel Continental. The Gestapo obviously hadn't traced the exploding loaves back to Herr Schmidt. In the dim and distant past, before the war, I also vaguely recalled a schoolboy match we'd played at the Zenith ground—it was a poky old dump with rickety wooden stands built before the Revolution.

'Is this Herr Schmidt one of ours?' I asked.

He frowned and tut-tutted.

'Steady on, son. All I can say is that this gentleman is doing his bit for former players—the food situation's pretty desperate; many are dying of starvation. So friend Schmidt is offering Dinamo players a bakery job. If you sign on, you and your mates won't be short of a crust, *and* you'll be able to play football again.'

I still looked baffled.

'But who is there to play?'

'Schmidt plans matches against Fascist sides—you know, Hungarians, Italians, Romanians, Slovaks, that sort of riff-raff. He's also arranging a match against Rukh,

119

nationalist hirelings from the city of Lvov. The final match is against a German team.'

'But why should the Nazis allow football matches?'

'Well, evidently, this Schmidt was singing the praises of our prewar football when some high-ranking Gestapo chief bet him we wouldn't stand a chance against properly-trained Europeans. They shook hands on it and drew up a fixture list.'

'What about Commissar Koch?'

It was an obvious question. No match could take place without Koch's say-so. And would he let his men play against subhumans like us?

'Koch's given it the nod. The word is that orders came down from the highest level.'

Comrade Danko put one finger under his nose and raised his right arm in a mock Nazi salute.

'Why should *we* agree?' I asked unsurely. 'What chance would our starving lads have against fit, well-trained soldiers?'

My question clearly rattled him. But I could see he knew I was right.

'We want the best side we can gather. Any victory over Fascism is a contribution to the war effort, remember that! Until the tide turns—and turn it will!—victory on the football field will show our people we *can* win, we *can* beat the Fascists. Even a small victory brings the hope of bigger victories to come!'

I changed tack. 'Will all of us be going back?'

'No, just seven of you. The two wounded lads will stay put until they've recovered. As for the girls, we need them here. Comrade Sasha is making Vera second-in-command. Sorry, Vova, it's a matter of where best to deploy resources on the war front.'

So Vera was a resource on the partisan front. I was a resource on the football front. She had to score hits. I had to score goals. Same thing really. As I left the bunker I promised to do my best.

It didn't take long to round up the gang. Igor came hobbling on makeshift crutches, but Borya was too ill to be moved. He'd caught a bullet in the spine and was due to go to a field hospital at Konotop—if they transferred him in time . . .

I broke the news.

Vera was unmoved. She was glad to remain, though naturally sorry to let me go: she was my Big Sister, after all. Her friend Maya was quite put out.

'You boys have it dead easy, you do! Just because you can kick a football. Well, I wouldn't swap my gun for a pig's bladder! You can't kick the enemy to death with football boots!'

She spat on her hands and rubbed them together, as if washing her hands of us; then she stomped off, snorting like a pig.

Far from feeling ashamed, we chosen few were excited and eager to get back to the game we loved. I told them of Herr Schmidt and the matches he'd lined up for us; we couldn't wait to get started. Though no one mentioned it, we weren't sorry to exchange our cold, wet, half-starved existence for the dry, warm bakery surrounded by the smell of baking bread and crusty rolls.

The hardest bit was saying goodbye to Igor. His smashed foot would never kick a ball again. He knew it. We knew it, though we mumbled reassuring promises:

'You'll join us as soon as your foot's mended.'

'We need you to beat the Fascists!'

Igor really would be missed. He'd been our leading goalscorer and a reserve for the Ukraine against the Spanish Basque team. He now stared down at his roughly bandaged right foot, his 'thunder-boot'. Then slowly he looked up with a forced smile. He was fighting back the tears when he muttered, 'Best of luck, lads. I'll work on my left foot.'

Abruptly, he twisted his crutches round and hobbled off.

It was several days later, in the dead of night, that the seven of us left the camp. We no longer had nimble Vanya to show the way—he'd moved on and, so we'd heard, shot himself when caught in an ambush. Now we were on our own.

Comrade Danko had shown us a rough pencil sketch full of dots, lines, and squiggles, indicating roads, woods, German bases, bogs and the River Dnieper. A large arrow pointed to Kiev.

All we knew about the Schmidt bakery was that it was in the south-west suburbs of the city. Nothing more.

I was appointed team captain and chief scout—on the strength of being Vera's brother!

If it hadn't been wartime, when you could get yourself killed at any time, our trek back would have been an adventure, rather like our prewar Pioneer hikes—without the drums, marching songs, and flags. But the hikes been good training for fording streams, map-reading, using the stars, and roughing it in the wild.

Since we had no weapons or other tell-tale evidence of partisan attachment—in case we got nabbed—we had to rely on our wits. If we'd been captured and submitted to a 'Fascist manicure', we'd surely have spilled the beans. It didn't bear thinking about.

As it was, we only had one really scary moment. As we were splashing through a stream, we heard low voices nearby; and by the sudden urgent cries and rushing feet, we knew they were on to us. From the harsh, throaty sounds, the voices were certainly *not* Ukrainian.

We froze in mid-stream, not daring to move, back or forward, for fear of alerting them. All we could do was hold our breath and hope they passed us by. Fat chance of that with the Man in the Moon laughing down.

The pounding and shouting were coming closer and closer. They were almost on us when, all at once, they stopped. We could scarcely credit our luck. To our amazement, we heard laughter and a few hearty curses, followed by heavy splashes coming towards us.

It was a herd of elk!

Good old Ukrainian hatstands. They'd been startled by intruders crashing into their forest bedroom, and they'd put the Germans off our scent. They saved our bacon.

Once the enemy was out of earshot, we made stealthy progress towards Kiev. After a while we sniffed water, lots of flowing water, the familiar, marshy catfish smell of the river, our Dnieper.

Once we reached its bank we knew we were as good as home.

All we had to do was follow its course.

25

In the city we had to be extra careful because of the curfew. Nine to nine. Anyone caught out of doors without a permit would be shot. No questions asked. Notices everywhere made that deathly clear.

So we shared a deserted boathouse with a big family of river rats; they eyed us hungrily . . . and we them.

Next morning we set off for the bakery. There was no hiding place in the open. But neither German soldiers, nor the local *Hilfi* police paid us much attention. To them we were just another gang of filthy ragamuffins roaming the streets for food. Whenever we spotted a checkpoint we doubled back and circled round it.

The city had changed beyond recognition in the ten months we'd been away. Our German guests had done their damnedest to turn it into a home-from-home. Shops that weren't boarded up had German names with prices marked in the strange *Karbowanek*. Street signs were all in German: 'Adolf Hitler Strasse. Reichskantzler Platz'. The unfamiliar stink of cigars and German sausage was in the air.

Civilians we passed were gaunt and haggard with sunken eyes—none looked up. It was as if they didn't want to see what was happening around them or were afraid of catching someone's eye. Some were pushing home-made carts carrying dead or nearly-dead bodies. No grief. No tears. Just blank, staring downturned faces. On living and dead alike.

In one square, hanging from lampposts, were six young men and women; they had placards tied with string about their necks.

'*WEGEN SABOTAGE WERDEN ZUM TODEN VERURTEILT*!'

Yakov, who knew Yiddish, translated for us:

'Sabotage is Punishable by Death!'

No one spoke. Each knew that hanging could be *our* fate. Today. Tomorrow. We hurried on.

Next minute we thought our end had come. As we turned a corner, we walked straight into a line of soldiers checking papers. They blocked the street, legs apart, guns at the hip. It was too late to turn and run: a party of *Hilfis* barred our escape route.

We had no papers. What's more, Tolya our goalie had a pocket knife—and carrying any weapon was punishable by death. For the first time we gave ourselves up for dead.

We were saved by the German sense of humour.

A ragged little urchin—he couldn't have been more than six or seven—was pushing a handcart along the road. It carried the dead body of a woman, her head flopping over the side. On seeing the soldiers, the boy dropped the cart and ran towards them, holding out his hands and crying, '*Yest! Yest hochoo!*'

To make them understand he put his little fists to his mouth and made eating signs.

We watched, our hearts beating fast, wondering what would happen. At first, we thought they'd gun him down. One burly soldier had stepped forward, training his gun on the scrawny figure. But another put a hand on his arm and said something loudly in German.

At that the soldiers burst out laughing and began mocking the starving boy. One pointed to the dead woman, presumably his mother, making sawing signs and chewing, as if to say: 'Eat her!'. Another, however, seemed to take pity on him. He went up to the little boy and squatted on his haunches.

'*Essen?*' he said kindly. '*Ja, Ja, warte auf, Ivan.*'

125

He went behind the sentry hut and soon returned with a paper bag. This he held out like a bag of groceries. With a smile, he shouted out, smacking his lips, *'Gut! Gut! Deutsche Scheisse.'*

The boy eagerly took the bag and opened it. We were beginning to think at least some Germans weren't so bad when the boy suddenly dropped the bag in horror. Its contents spilled out over the cobblestones.

The stink of shit told us what *'Deutsche Scheisse'* meant.

The Germans and *Hilfis* couldn't contain themselves. They laughed so much, they doubled up, tears rolling down their red cheeks. The incident, though, saved us from certain death: we were able to slip through the *Hilfi* line and evade the road block. It was a near thing.

'Saved by a bag of shit!' muttered Tolya.

The bakery found us rather than us finding it.

The strong yeasty smell of baked bread wafted through the air, leading us by the nose. Nostrils up, mouths watering, bellies rumbling, we followed our noses to a drab grey concrete building fronted by a cobblestone yard full of delivery vans. Above the gates was a freshly-painted black fretwork sign:

OTTO SCHMIDT BÄKEREI

Odd home for footballers. But we barely gave that a thought. The lovely mouth-watering smell was tormenting our stomachs: our one desire was to sink our teeth into fresh crusty bread.

Boldly I led the way across the yard and into the bakery, as if clocking on for the midday shift. None of the drivers, stackers, tray bearers gave us a second glance.

'Where's Herr Schmidt's office?' I asked an elderly man sweeping the long corridor.

Without looking up, he muttered, 'Up the stairs, turn right, end of passage.'

We climbed the stone steps and made our way to a dark-green door marked 'Herr O. Schmidt'. I knocked.

A young woman in white cap and smock opened the door, just wide enough to see out without us seeing in.

'*Was wilst Du?* What do you want?'

I wasn't sure what name to give.

'We're footballers.'

It was probably a daft thing to say. As if to make the point I thrust my chest out, pulled my shoulders back and chin in. My muddy face, uncombed hair, and ragged clothes seemed to amuse her.

'And I'm the Empress of Russia,' she said in Ukrainian.

I tried again.

'We're from Dinamo Kiev; we were told to report to Herr Schmidt.'

She obviously was no football fan. What's more, she was tiring of this time-wasting conversation.

'This is a bakery, sonny. It makes bread for the German army. We don't bake footballs; nor do we need bone-headed doughnuts. Clear off.'

The door slammed shut.

Just then a tall, well-dressed man in suit and bow tie came striding towards us. He smelt deliciously of bread rolls. What's more he was smiling—a floury smile.

'Hello, lads,' he said warmly. Turning to Yakov, he said, 'Livshits, isn't it? And . . . ' He searched our faces . . . 'young Grechko?'

I was flattered. Yakov wasn't so sure: he wondered whether to claim mistaken identity.

'Er, yes, sir. Rather, no, sir. Yakov . . . Ulyanov.'

The tall man laughed.

'Ah, Comrade Lenin, I presume! Your *nom de guerre* . . . A wartime alias. Fine, fine. As long as your football's better than Lenin's. Anyway, come in, come in. Good to meet you.'

He threw open the door and swept inside, leaving a trail of flour as he went. We followed in his wake as if behind our captain on to the pitch. The woman in white stood up. But her polite smile instantly turned sour the moment he'd passed into an inner room. We gave her a triumphant grin, the one we give opposing fans on scoring a goal.

'Sit yourselves down, my lads.'

There were only two chairs in the cosy oak-panelled inner room: a battered leather chair behind the desk, and a covered metal chair up front. We all sat cross-legged on the carpeted floor, afraid of dirtying the spotless chair cover. Meanwhile, he poked his head round the door and called cheerily, 'Olechka, some poppyseed rolls for my team.'

In hushed tones he whispered, turning back to us, 'Poppyseed rolls are reserved for the Gestapo—but we're permitted to keep the crumbly, misshapen ones!'

He laughed. His Ukrainian had just a trace of an accent—the roll of his 'r's.

You'd have thought, as a German, he'd be strutting around, treating us as the soldiers had treated the little cart pusher. But no, he shook our grubby hands, leaned against the front of his desk, and explained his plans like a coach talking tactics before a game.

'How skinny you are. Dear me, dear me. I must fatten you up, like the witch fattening up Hansel and Gretel, eh? You must have a job, nothing too strenuous; I'll get you into shape.'

He really did inspect us like the witch sizing up poor Hansel.

'I've already got six or seven players on the payroll, some from Dinamo, some Lokomotiv. We call ourselves *Start*; sounds harmless enough. A new Start, eh? They've banned us from using the name Dinamo because of its secret police connections.

'I've rented a pitch behind the bakery, the old Zenith Stadium; I've patched it up, cut the grass, painted the benches. It'll do. We don't have much time though. Our first match is a week from today.'

He looked witch-like at us once more and sighed.

'Our first opponents are my Fascist pals from west Ukraine, *Rukh*.'

As he uttered the words 'Fascist pals', he gave us a wink, saying quietly, 'We'll beat the shit out of them, eh, lads?'

His excited talk was interrupted by Olechka's rolls.

'Say hello to our famous footballers,' he said proudly to his secretary.

'I've already met them, sir,' she said, clearly not wishing to dirty her hands on the scruff-bags littering the floor.

Noticing her wrinkled nose, Herr Schmidt smiled and said gently, 'If only you knew, Olya, how proud you'll be of them one day.'

She gave us a look that spoke volumes: 'You must be stark raving mad!'

We thought so too.

26

Over the next week, we slept in dry, clean beds in the bakery dormitory; in the daytime we did light work as tray stackers—and we put some flesh on our bones through eating so much bread that it was soon coming out of our ears. Oh, for a hunk of pork fat, raw onion, and pickled cucumber!

The Schmidt Bakery had a strict rule: you could eat bread on the premises, but on *no* account take any out. Not only would you be shot on the spot, you'd endanger Herr Schmidt's position. And if we lost him, the next boss might be the Gestapo.

Every afternoon and evening we trained under the watchful eye of our old coach. Ivan Ivanovich had been smuggled into the bakery with false papers as a delivery man. But that wasn't all: we were joining six former first-team players. Crucially, they included the prewar Ukrainian goalkeeper Kolya Trusevich, winger Makar Goncharenko, and Dinamo captain Mikol Melnik.

All in all, we now numbered a baker's dozen—thirteen; most fitting for a baker's team.

By the following Sunday we were beginning to knit together as a team; not everyone played in their best position, but at least we had a seasoned goalie, nippy striker (me!), fairly solid defence, and two speedy wingers. We knew nothing about *Rukh*, the side we were due to play at three o'clock that afternoon.

All we'd been told was that they were from Lvov, fought for the Germans and had welcomed the Fascists into the Ukraine. That was enough incentive for us to beat them. In our eyes they were traitors, Fascist hirelings, bandits who outdid the Nazis in cruelty.

Perhaps the city authorities couldn't bank on their Ukrainian allies giving us a good hiding; for they were playing the match behind closed doors. No civilian was allowed into the stadium. All the same, a few hundred soldiers and police filled the sunny side of the ground as we took the pitch.

Germany's allies the Italians were the easiest to spot because they made more noise than the Germans and other Fascist troops, like Slovaks and Hungarians. Of course, *Rukh* had their own supporters, waving yellow and blue flags and Swastika pennants. To their dismay, there wasn't much love lost on 'traitors'; even on their own side, among the Italians above all. So we were pleasantly surprised to find many fans cheering us. Even a few Germans shouted '*Russland!* Dinamo!', perhaps because our colours were German as well as Dinamo: white shirts and navy-blue shorts. Our opponents sported yellow and blue.

I played inside right, feeding our winger Makar Goncharenko and shooting whenever I could. As if to show their disapproval, however, the skies opened just before kick off and poured down angry rain, drenching spectators and players alike.

Not that it dampened our spirits. We vowed to beat— no, trounce!—these traitors from west Ukraine. They hardly knew what hit them! Within twenty minutes we were 3–0 up; in the second half they ran out of steam and guts, surrendering 14–1. *Rukh* was whistled off the pitch.

One up to us. Bring on the next team.

On successive Sundays, we took on and beat Hungarians, Romanians, Slovaks, and Italians. Not by the odd goal, but by five or six clear goals. Herr Schmidt could hardly conceal his joy as he greeted each victory. He also cleaned up from his Nazi friends on big match bets.

Record so far: Five games. Five wins. Thirty-two goals for, three against. I had scored eight.

Our final match was scheduled for the second Sunday in August. We were to play a team billed as *Flakelf* (Germany). We assumed it would be a collection of off-duty anti-aircraft German servicemen in and around Kiev. But we sniffed trouble in the air.

At the start of the week, Herr Schmidt came into our changing room after training.

'I have some news for you,' he said gravely. 'Hitler himself has taken an interest in the result of Sunday's match. He's no soccer fan; he prefers kicking heads to kicking balls. But he won't tolerate a single German defeat, even on the football field. Not only that, he has a point to prove to Stalin.'

In a quiet voice, he continued, 'My German friends tell me he has instructed *Luftwaffe* boss Goering to assemble a tough team of professionals to send to Kiev. You are up against the might of German football.'

Coach couldn't contain himself.

'All the better! We'll lick them! Then we can tell the world we defeated the best the Nazis could throw at us.'

Turning to us, seated along the walls, he said grimly, 'Lads, you've got a big responsibility on your shoulders.'

'The odds are stacked against us,' warned the bakery chief. 'As referee they've appointed Paul Blobel, the notorious commando captain. It was his *Sonderkommando* unit that carried out the Babi Yar massacre. So expect no favours from him. He's under instructions from the Führer to ensure German victory.

'One last thing. So confident are they of winning—and winning well—they're printing programmes advertising the match and opening up the stadium to the public—to watch Christians being fed to the lions; or is it lion cubs being fed to the Christians? The match is to be broadcast all along the front, to Russia and back to Germany.'

For the first time we saw defeat staring us in the face. How could we overcome top German pros, fit, strong, well-fed—not to mention a Nazi butcher as ref?

'Right,' said Coach, spitting on his hands, 'all the more reason why we *must* win. So we're going to train twice as hard. And at the end of the day, we have eleven men, they have eleven men.'

'Wrong,' said Herr Schmidt. 'They have twelve; you forget the referee!'

Coach had to have the last word: 'He who wins will be he who wants victory more . . .'

However, something happened next day that took everyone's mind off the match. About mid-morning, we heard a great crashing and shouting coming from the yard. Suddenly, the doors burst open and in rushed a squad of black-uniformed Gestapo troops led by 'mad dog' Koch himself.

A pale-faced Herr Schmidt was escorted from his office and forced to look on as the Gestapo lined up his employees against the bakery wall—secretaries, cleaners, drivers, dough-makers, delivery men, and us stackers. We bunched at one end.

With guns trained on us, Koch mounted a wooden box in the middle of the yard, brandishing his pistol and screaming so hard we thought he'd burst a blood vessel. He had appointed himself Judge, Jury, and Executioner. Now he read the Riot Act: Charge, Verdict, Sentence.

The translation was brief and to the point.

'Saboteurs at the bakery wilfully put ground glass into loaves sent to the Gestapo. Three officers died, ten are in hospital. One hundred bakery employees are to be shot forthwith . . . unless the saboteurs come forward.'

No one moved.

Angrily, Koch waved his pistol-holding gloved hand towards a senior officer. He was to select the condemned by pointing to every fifth man in the line.

As the officer walked down the line of men, he started counting: *'Ein, zwei, drei, vier, fünf.'* Tap on the shoulder. Then, again, *'Ein, zwei, drei, vier, fünf.'* Tap on shoulder. At each tap the unfortunate victim was dragged out by two soldiers and made to stand four paces in front of the others.

It didn't need a knowledge of German to understand our fate. It was simple maths.

Each of us desperately tried to count along the line. Were we the unlucky fifth? Dear God, let me be second or third, somewhere in the middle. In the football team I was No. 9, lucky nine. Let me be nine!

My prayers were answered. The officer merely glanced at me and barked 'zwei'. OK. I'll settle for the No. 2 shirt. Saved!

To our horror, three of our team were selected for the firing squad: Alex Klimenko, Kolya Trusevich, and Yakov Livshits-Ulyanov.

It was bad enough losing a hundred fellow workers, but to lose our team mates was a devastating blow. Apart from the horror of their execution, we knew we couldn't sacrifice three of our best players and win the match.

Herr Schmidt knew so too. He was faced by a dilemma. Should he plead for his players? If he did, and he succeeded, it would mean three other workers being shot in their place. We looked on, holding our breath, as he stepped forward to speak to Commissar Koch.

As a respected German with friends in high places—it was rumoured he spent much of his profit on handsome gifts to influential Nazis—Otto Schmidt was not someone to brush aside. But Koch was answerable to Hitler alone. All the same, from his soap-box, the stocky red-faced Koch bent an ear to the tall, grey-haired bakery boss. They had a hurried, heated conversation.

We learned from Schmidt later that he had to pay a large bribe to Koch to secure the players' release; but he had also warned that German victory in Sunday's match would be worthless if everyone knew they were playing a much-weakened team, deprived of top players before the match.

Koch gave in. The three players were pushed back in line; and no further victims were chosen.

At an order from Koch, we were marched to the other side of the yard and forced to watch as the Gestapo executioners lined up twenty paces from the condemned employees. They raised their rifles.

On the command *'Feuer!'*, they fired bullets into ninety-seven bodies until all had fallen, sprawled in pools of blood.

'Let that be a lesson to you all!' screamed Koch.

It was a lesson all right. It made us determined to win—for the sake of our dead comrades.

27

In the fourteen months of Nazi occupation, German signs and swastikas had gone up on every highway; helmeted German soldiers strutted through the cobblestone streets. That we got used to. What was hard to stomach were the creepy-crawlies who constantly appeared out of the woodwork, Kievans who hated Jews and communists, who collaborated with the enemy against their own people.

One such weasel turned up at our training ground on the day before the match. I knew him slightly—Edward Kuts, half German. I'd played football with him when I first joined the Juniors. Funny that: he was a coward even then, scared of a hard tackle, yet elbowed you in the face when the ref's back was turned.

Anyway, this fellow barged into our changing room; he was wearing the yellow and blue *Hilfi* armband. All the same, he acted pally, as if he was on our side, rooting for us against the Germans. Suddenly, he recognized Yakov and his smile faded.

'Livshits!' he hissed. 'Germans don't play with Jews!'

A deathly silence descended. Yakov was ours. Before the invasion no one had given a thought to him being Jewish. We had Tartars, Russians, Jews, Ukrainians, even a German in our prewar squad. Nobody ever saw them as being anything but part of the team.

Coach's rasping voice cut through the tension.

'Get out! This is a football team, not a Hitler admiration society!'

The traitor glared from Coach to Yakov, and spat out,

'You'll pay for insulting our Führer! You—communist, and you—filthy Jew!'

With that he turned on his heel and left.

Once out on the pitch in the warmth of early August, we breathed in the fresh smell of grass and bindweed, of greased leather and honest sweat. For a while we could forget the war, the Nazis, and their hirelings; we were playing the game we loved.

The stone terraces rang hollowly to our shouts, the goalposts were netless, the blue sky was dotted with grey barrage balloons and dark warplanes. A group of old women with clumps of birch sticks were sweeping the track around the pitch in preparation for tomorrow's match.

We sprinted and leapt in the air, scored goals galore, ran off our nervous energy, puffed and beamed through veils of sweat. Yakov set me up for two goals, and I returned the compliment.

After a couple of hours Coach blew his whistle and we all trooped off. The showers had no hot water, just a dribble of cold, brackish liquid that hardly wet our heads. We didn't mind.

'Well done, lads,' said Coach. 'Early night tonight: be fit for the Big Match tomorrow. Assemble at midday.'

Notices had gone up all over the city advertising the game. It was billed in German and Ukrainian as a 'Grudge Match'—as if the Germans were to take revenge for the defeat of their Fascist allies.

I read the large poster on the bakery wall.

FOOTBALL

REVENGE

START   VS.   FLAKELF
(Ukraine)   (Germany)

FUSSBALL SPIEL

REVANCHE

Zenith Stadium

24 Kerosene Street

KICK OFF 3 p.m.

Entrance Free

Our thirteen players were listed by name. No names under Flakelf, just the words 'Strengthened Team'.

They need not have bothered. Even those who detested football would have given their back teeth to see their side thrash the Germans. They were not to know what the Germans had planned: a crooked referee and a crack team flown in specially from Berlin!

That night the entire team was in bed by ten o'clock. Yakov, who slept by the door in the bed next to mine, switched off the dormitory light. Next thing we knew the door flew open and the light came back on.

Standing in the doorway were four thick-necked soldiers, guns pointing at us. Our 'old pal' Edward, the informer, stood by Yakov's bed, a look of hatred twisting his ugly features.

'That's the Jew!' he snarled.

It was all over after a brief struggle. Two of the men grabbed the wriggling Yakov and frogmarched him out and down the stairs. It happened so quickly none of us had time to move—even if we'd dared. Only when they'd gone did we jump out of bed, rush to the windows, and peer out into the gloom. We were just in time to see Yakov being bundled into the back of a truck.

All at once, I heard someone call my name.

'Vova! Win for me!'

Win what? The football match? The war?

My head was still swimming with the previous night's events when I reported at the ground next day. Of course, Yakov was missing. We replaced him with the 'dodgy' Komarov borrowed from *Rukh*. But Coach's calm, if ashen, face gave us some comfort. No one dared mention our missing team mate.

'Right, lads, listen carefully, I don't care who hears— my days are numbered anyway. But I *do* care about you.

You are *my* players, *my* team, *my* family. Remember: this is the biggest match of your lives.'

We did some limbering up, loosening our muscles and joints. Then we went for a 'light' lunch—fried bread, black and white slices of bread, fresh rolls, bread pudding. Over lunch, Herr Schmidt came to wish us well; he too made no mention of Yakov. Nor, strangely, did he urge us to win.

It was just after two o'clock when we returned to the changing room. Herr Schmidt had prepared a little surprise for us—a brand new kit. Not our normal Dinamo colours of black and white—the Germans had taken that for themselves. But red shirts, white shorts, and red stockings: our Soviet—communist—team colours.

As we were proudly pulling on the new kit, the black-suited referee walked in. So this was the butcher of Babi Yar! He was a small, completely bald-headed man with a thin moustache, quite unremarkable apart from his staring eyes. They were black and beady, like an eagle's, and seemed to pierce right through you.

In hesitant Russian, he said, 'You know rules?'

Coach looked offended.

'Of course we know the bloody rules. Make sure your lot does!'

I had rarely heard Coach swear; perhaps he no longer cared about insulting Germans.

'No, you not understand,' said the Gestapo referee steadily. 'Not football rules. War rules.'

He could tell by our puzzled looks that we didn't know what he was talking about. It had to be spelled out.

'You will lose,' he said.

'Oh no we won't!' cried Coach. 'We're going to bloody well win!'

The referee gave him a pitying look, as one would a gibbering idiot. Drawing a thin finger across his throat, he said coldly, 'Win—you die. Lose—you live . . . .'

To stunned silence, he turned and left us to deal with this bombshell.

The Match of Death!

We couldn't take it in. Could football really be a matter of life or death? For several minutes no one said a word. It was numbing. We didn't want to die, we wanted to play football. Yet no one dared say the unsayable:

'To live we had to lose.'

To each his own thoughts as we tied our bootlaces, fussed over our shinpads, combed a parting in our hair, bounced the practice balls, anything to break the silence and occupy ourselves without having to speak.

It was Coach who said the inevitable, in a roundabout way.

'Best of luck, comrades,' he said before we took the field. 'I won't be seeing you again—I've served my purpose. Don't let me down. Play fairly. And remember: even if we don't win *this* battle, we'll win the war.'

He hugged each of us in turn, tears rolling down his rugged cheeks.

As the German referee walked ahead of both sides down the tunnel and on to the pitch, the roar that greeted us lifted our spirits. For the first time that day, it stirred feelings of pride in our country.

We could feel shame later.

For the moment I savoured the sheer joy of seeing and hearing those ten thousand Kiev fans on three sides of the ground shouting, 'DEE—NA—MO! DEE—NA—MO!!'

The eleven players in each team lined up in the centre for the national anthems. First came *'Deutschland über Alles'*, which was met in almost total silence. Only the German team and solid ranks of Gestapo officers in the main stand made an effort to fill the air with song. Their officer allies from Hungary, Romania, and Italy seemed not to know the words, though they held up their right arms and, at the end, shouted 'Heil, Hitler!'

Then, as massed voices got ready to sing the Soviet national anthem, over the loudspeaker came the strains of the prewar Ukrainian hymn, 'The Great Gates of Kiev'.

After a brief moment of surprise, the music was drowned out by full-throated voices singing our proper anthem:

'So, Comrades, come rally, and the last fight will we face . . .'

There was nothing the Germans could do about it, even though the track was ringed by soldiers with dogs and guns pointing at the crowd.

The Match of Death kicked off.

28

Our hearts weren't in it. You could tell that right from the start. We were weighed down by the threat of death. Naturally, we were slow on the turn, half-hearted in attack, unwilling to chase and harry. I was scared of shooting in case the ball ended up in the net!

If fear weren't bad enough, we were up against twelve men—the German team *and* the German referee. The match was only five minutes old when our centre forward outpaced the last defender; he would surely have scored. But an arm grabbed him round the neck and wrestled him to the ground.

Penalty!

We all stopped, expecting the whistle.

A happy excited buzz went round the ground.

The Italian contingent was on its feet, pointing to the penalty spot and screaming 'PENALTY!'

But the stony-faced man in black was waving play on, as if his arms were rolling up a carpet.

When Igor our captain muttered 'Cheat' as the ref backpedalled, the Gestapo officer halted the game and called Igor over. With one thin finger to his lips and an arm pointing to the dressing room, the warning was clear.

First, we couldn't expect fair play.

Second, we could like it or lump it: if we complained we'd be sent off.

Bucked by the referee's blatant bias, our opponents tripped, elbowed, pushed, and ankle-tapped whenever we had the ball. They were bent on winning by foul means, not fair. They had the ref in their pocket.

Despite the odds stacked against us, we fought on, defending doggedly, our backs to the wall. Yet we never resorted to dirty tactics. We couldn't play football any other way. Fair play was in our blood.

We held out for thirty minutes. We were even thinking we might hold on for a draw to the bitter end. Then, during a German attack, a high cross came into our penalty area. Kolya, our goalie, caught the ball cleanly just under the bar and clutched it safely to his chest.

What he didn't expect was an express train to barge into him. Their burly centre forward came charging into Kolya, knocking him to the ground, then lashing out with his boot. Thud! Thud! Thud! The sickening thud of bone on leather could be heard high in the stands.

Bravely Kolya hung on tightly to the ball. But the German wouldn't let up: he was set on kicking the ball *and* Kolya's head into the back of the net.

We heard a stomach-churning 'CR-RACK!'

As I leaned anxiously over our goalie, his eyes disappeared up under his bruised lids and his head lolled back.

At last, the ball rolled loose. And it was booted into the net.

One–Nil.

The referee was pointing upfield.

We couldn't believe it.

They had knocked out our goalie, broken his jaw by the sound of things, and kicked the ball out of his hands into the net.

And the referee had given a goal.

A terrible hush hung like a sinister cloud over the ground. Kiev people were used to being beaten up, dragged from their beds in the middle of the night, tortured and killed. That was war.

But this was a game of football. A *game*. A *game* which

had rules that everyone had to abide by. The *game* had a referee to make sure players kept those rules.

This was something different. It wasn't a game we recognized.

We felt crushed, helpless. So did our fans.

But there was someone who would not be crushed. If we were prepared to play to the whistle, he wasn't! Coach was dancing up and down on the touchline in a fury, wagging his long finger in the linesman's face. We never discovered whether the linesman spoke our language or not. He must have by the way his face turned from salmon pink to beetroot red as Coach's curses rained down on him.

At last, a long blast on the whistle brought play to a halt. Not to attend to the unconscious Kolya, but for a squad of black-uniformed Gestapo police to grab Ivan Ivanovich, pin his arms behind his back and march him off down the tunnel.

While this was happening, four of us carried Kolya off the pitch to our worried sponge man. Makar gently pulled off his green jersey and put it on himself.

'I'll take over in goal, lads—just till Kolya's fit again.'

'Fit again!' With a broken jaw and blood streaming from a nasty head gash—not to mention eyes closed in a dead faint! We even wondered whether he was a gonner . . .

A sharp blast from the referee's whistle recalled us to the kick-off. We were now down to ten men.

Like sharks scenting blood, the Germans came at us, boots flying, fists flailing—knowing they could get away with blue murder. As it was, we were half-starved, weak, and mostly teenage runts—our natural growth had been stunted by war.

They were well-fed, well-trained professionals—rough and tough into the bargain, handpicked by their Air Force Chief, Goering—to flatten us like a steamroller.

It was no contest, especially with the one-eyed referee.

We gave ground, avoided heavy tackles, got rid of the ball the moment we received it. By half-time the Germans were leading 2–0 and the crowd was silent, unable to comprehend—all except the German soldiers and police. Even their allies were starting to whistle at our cowardly display. They clearly wanted us to beat the arrogant Nazis.

29

There was no Coach in the changing room at the break. Ivan Ivanovich had already been led away to the nearby barracks. As a communist, he had always known what his fate would be—once he'd served his purpose.

We missed him badly.

There was no one to give us confidence, point out our mistakes, change tactics or formation.

There was also no sign of our injured goalie. Perhaps he'd died of his injuries and been taken off to the morgue? No one could tell us. Or no one *wanted* to tell us.

We sat in silence, avoiding each other's eyes, sipping cold tea left in a tea pot on the samovar in the corner. We were glad when the ten-minute break was up and we had to run out into daylight once more.

The second half went much like the first, and the Kiev fans showed their disappointment and disgust. No longer did they get behind us, urging us on. Now they were on our backs, telling us what they thought of our feeble efforts.

Midway through the half, our captain limped over and handed me his armband.

'Vova, take over as captain. I'm crocked. I'll hobble out on the wing; with any luck I'll run it off.'

I was pleased, yet surprised. After all, I was the youngest in the side. The game had halted for attention to a German hurt in the tackle with our captain. During the stoppage, I heard a cry from the crowd.

'Vova! Call yourself a patriot! Get stuck in, for God's sake!'

I couldn't believe it. I searched the sea of faces on the

other side of the touchline. Yes, there she was . . . Mum! There were three of them together. How? Why?

Mum, Vera, Dad—like old times.

Mum and Vera were on their feet, shouting, waving their arms, willing me to play well. Dad was silent, holding his head in his hands.

I made up my mind.

I ran from the touchline to our goalmouth, calling the team together.

'Listen, Team,' I said breathlessly. 'We can't let the fans down.'

You only had to look at those haggard, hopeful faces in the crowd to realize what defeat would mean. On the other hand, if we were to win . . .

'Better die in hope than live in shame!' I said.

'Right!'

I heard a strange half-strangled voice behind me. It was Kolya, our goalie, his head swathed in bandages. A broad elastic band from head to chin clamped his jaw in place, making it hard for him to speak. Yet nothing was going to stop him from muttering, 'If any of you cowards want to lose, keep my green jersey and I'll play out. At least I'll break a few legs before they break me.'

Makar handed him back his jersey with a smile. Coach had ordered us to play fairly, so we couldn't risk Kolya running riot on the field . . .

But our mood had changed. The tide had turned. When the game restarted we threw ourselves into the match, chased every ball, and tackled like terriers. The Germans must have wondered what hit them.

Within five minutes we scored—to the delight of our fans. Fifteen minutes remained for us to draw level. The crowd willed us on, chanted, sang, shouted, cursed the Germans—Thank God those Germans didn't understand our language.

Now that I was desperate to score, I couldn't! I hit the post with one pile-driver, headed against the bar when I should have scored, and then shot hopefully from a long way out. As luck would have it, the ball caught the heel of their centre half and flew into the corner of the net.

2–2.

The crowd went wild. Even the nationalists were on their feet cheering.

My first thought was of Coach. Could he hear the roar from his cell? I was sure he could!

With one minute to go the game seemed all over—a draw. Our lives were saved. The referee blew his whistle as Kolya was challenged roughly in catching the ball. We thought he'd blown for the end of the game. But to everyone's astonishment he was pointing to the spot.

Penalty!

Even some of the German team seemed embarrassed at the decision after such a tough game. We'd earned even their respect.

Amid a cascade of whistles, their captain cooly aimed hard and low for the corner. Yet Kolya took off as if he had springs in his heels, caught the ball and, in one movement, threw it upfield to me.

With no one for support, I raced forward on my own. Three defenders stood between me and the goal. I tapped the ball through one man's legs and tore down the right wing, drawing the second defender. Then I cut inside to take on the other. As they converged in a sandwich from either side, I drew back the ball with my foot, flicked it up and over the defenders, then nipped in between them.

My speed took me through the tackle as they crashed into each other. That left me one-on-one with the goalkeeper.

For a split second I lost my nerve. Our team's lives rested on my shot. Then, all at once, Yakov's words flashed through my brain: 'Win for me!'

'I will, Yakov, I will!'

And I did. The ball flew into the top corner of the net, past the keeper's despairing dive.

It all happened so fast the German referee hadn't had time to blow his whistle for full time. Now he was standing still like a statue, uncertain what to do. It was only when the German captain placed the ball on the centre spot that he gave the goal.

The fans danced and sang and cheered as if we'd won the war. In a way we had. The Match of Death had turned into the Match of Life for the thousands . . . and the millions.

We *could* win. We *did* win. We *will* win.

Postscript

That is my story. I'm glad I've finished it before they come for me. I'm not afraid to die. I'd do it all over again just to see the joy on the faces of those fans.

Come to think of it . . . I *was* in the right place at the right time.